The Skeleton and the Lantern

MOTOMYSTERIES

BOOK 1

THE SKELETON AND THE LANTERN
© 2019 Sherri Kukla
Published by S&S Publishing
www.sherrikukla.com

ISBN: 9781697455281

COVER PHOTOGRAPHY
Motorcycle/Lantern/Skeleton - *Shutterstock*
Sand Car: Robert Jones at California's Dumont Dunes, November 2017
Neal Rideout Photo | www.fe135.com

Trust in the L*ORD* *with all your heart*
And do not lean on your own understanding.
Proverbs 3:5

In loving honor of my greatest
prayer warrior and champion
My Mother
Juanita Noah, Servant of God
12/17/34 - 7/12/19

For my granddaughter Summer
She encouraged me not to give up.
If not for her, the book would never have been completed.

MotoMysteries

Visit www.sherrikukla.com

for updates on new books

Prologue

How could I be dying already? I'm not done living.

"I know I'm only ten, but I'm serious, Dad. Someday I'm going to help boys, like that man in the movie did!" Was it really 60 years ago I said that?

My dad was right. He said the dream was too big.

It's not that I mind dying. It's my dream dying with me that hurts.

"Grandpa?"

Max, I wish I could talk to you.

"Grandpa, you're crying!" I hear the sadness.

"Grandpa . . ."

His voice is fading. Where is he going?

But wait, maybe it's not him leaving. It's me. I'm the one leaving.

"Don't forget the dream, Max." I try to get the words out, but my mouth won't work.

"Dad!" Max sounded excited. "Come in here! Grandpa talked to me!"

"No, son. Grandpa hasn't talked in days."

"He did, Dad. He said, 'Don't forget the dream, Max.'"

I wanted to jump for joy. God let me talk one last time. The dream won't die with me.

I can go now. Suddenly, I am jumping for joy.

The angels are taking me home.

CHAPTER 1

Jeremiah

Thirty years later

"Stop the car, Dad! There's a man hanging off the power station!"

Even though we were flying along the highway, I expected my dad to slam the brakes on right away so we could hop out and help that poor man. But my dad took his time on the narrow two-lane road. It seemed like forever before he found a safe spot to pull over.

I jumped out of the car before it came to a complete stop and ran over the rocky hills to get to the power station. We've seen it a billion times driving to the desert, but I never imagined we'd be rescuing a man in danger there some day.

Dad caught up with me just as I got close enough to realize my mistake. My very big mistake.

"Jeremiah! You risked our safety for a prank."

"Sorry, Dad. It looked like a real man as we whizzed by."

I watched the dummy flopping around in the breeze. Oops.

Back at the car we heard a horn honking. A white-haired guy in an old truck blew by us, missing our truck only by inches.

"Where did that idiot come from?" I knew that shook my dad up because normally he wouldn't call someone a name. At least not in front of me.

"I saw a motorcycle in his truck." It wouldn't help, but it was all I could think of.

"Well, I sure hope we don't run into him down there." Dad shook his head. "I doubt he is any safer in the dirt than on the pavement."

We were on our way to the desert to ride our dirt bikes and check out some land my parents planned to buy. "Hey, Dad, I hope that guy wasn't in a big hurry because he wants our land! He better not ruin it for us!"

Our long-time family dream was about to happen. Not dirt bike riding, but buying land out here. Riding motorcycles has been going on in my family for generations. Well, if you count me, my dad, his dad and his dad before that.

"Not likely." Dad checked the mirrors as he pulled back onto the road.

We had driven this way many times in my life because camping in Dry Brook – that's what they called the town we loved – was our number one, favorite family activity. Usually my mom and sister came too. We would bring our big toy hauler trailer. They call it that because there's room for the off-road toys and for sleeping. But this time we were doing a guys-only trip and roughing it.

"Minnesota!" I shouted, distracting my dad which isn't a good idea on a narrow winding road with an idiot ahead of us.

"What are you talking about?" He kept his eyes on the road and sighed like he just wanted to get there with no more surprises.

"That's where the idiot was from!"

"Jeremiah, don't call people names. I shouldn't have said that."

"Oh, okay." We went through this conversation every time an idiot, oops, I mean bad driver, passed us on the road. Dad would get upset, yell at the driver, then tell me later he was setting a bad example for me and that I shouldn't call people names.

"So how do you know?"

"Know what?" He confused me, because I had been thinking about Dad's habit of calling people names and then telling me not to call names. I thought he meant how did I know about that habit.

"How do you know he's from Minnesota?"

"I saw his license plate as he passed."

"Well, he's heading in the right direction. I hope he keeps driving and makes it there in one piece."

I never thought about this little highway leading to Minnesota. But I suppose if you headed east long enough, you could get almost anywhere from California.

We weren't expecting to see many people in Dry Brook on this camping trip. The weekends were the crowded times in the off-road park.

I was home schooled so I could go motorcycle riding anytime. Sometimes I brought my schoolwork with me. This time I did extra work for a week to have fun on our trip without schoolwork to worry about.

I couldn't wait to live down here. I'd be able to ride every day. But I'm getting ahead of myself.

Chapter 2

Millie

"Millicent! What kind of name is that?" Millie stormed through the house, banging the bathroom door shut behind her. She always went there to hide.

"Millie, please." Her mother's soft voice called out as she followed her and knocked on the door. "Let's talk."

"There's nothing to talk about." Millie yelled from inside. "It isn't fair! Dad took Jeremiah and not me and it's because you guys never wanted a girl, anyway. That's why Jeremiah gets to have all the fun!"

The ranting gave way to sniffling and then tears.

"Millie, please come out so we can talk."

Mom waited until the door opened but Millie wouldn't look her in the eyes. Her head hung low and long hair covered her face. She was still holding the crumpled up envelope with the court paperwork.

This time when Mom held her arms out Millie didn't pull away. She hugged her mother, burying her head in her mom's chest, letting the tears flow.

"This isn't about Jeremiah, is it?"

"Huh-uh." Her voice sounded muffled.

Mom led her into the kitchen where the smell of homemade chocolate chip cookies wafted from the oven. "Milk, tea or ginger ale?" Mom asked as she removed the cookies.

While Millie munched on a cookie and drank ice cold soda, Mom picked up the envelope and removed the paper. "You wouldn't even have seen this if you had been doing your schoolwork instead of going through my mail."

Millie ignored the kind reprimand and mimicked "In the matter of Millicent C. Reginald, a ward of the State blah blah blah." She

9

talked around a mouthful of cookie. "Millicent! Yuck and double yuck!"

Mom hugged her. "You're our daughter now and all this legal stuff isn't your concern. Next time stay out of my mail and save yourself some grief."

"Why is it taking so long to finish my adoption? There is no reason they should keep listening to that woman!" She picked up a cookie but then put it down again, hanging her head, then slamming her fist on the table. "She obviously doesn't want to be a mother. She never did one thing they told her to in six years."

Mom patted her shoulder. "And none of that is news to you. Why is it hitting you so hard today?"

"Because I wanted to go riding with Dad instead of doing stupid Social Studies!"

"Don't you think Jeremiah would have rather gone to the movies yesterday with you and Dad than doing schoolwork?" Mom stood and cleared the table. "Besides Dad left a surprise for you."

"Really?"

"As soon as your schoolwork is complete, you can go through the box he left for you. He said you've been asking about it."

The box! Millie couldn't believe she would finally get to look through it.

"Let me at that schoolwork!" She jumped up and disappeared from the kitchen.

Chapter 3

Jeremiah

We arrived at our destination without any more problems or unexpected stops. We were unloading the motorcycles when I heard a truck roaring along the dirt road nearby.

Oh, no! It was our friend from the highway. The idiot.

My dad seemed totally unaware. He was adjusting the motorcycle chain and getting his bike ready to ride. I don't know if it's what the adults call denial or if he just didn't realize the guy was heading right for us.

Sure enough, the guy pulled up next to us. Before my dad looked up, the guy shouted, "Holy buckets! I can't believe anyone else is out here today!"

I would have loved to see the look on my dad's face, but I was standing behind him.

Even if I hadn't seen the guy's license plate, I knew by that greeting he wasn't from around here.

"I'm Mike!" He shouted again. I don't know why he was so loud because he was standing right by us when he got out of his truck. "Minnesota Mike they call me!" He had a huge smile, like he just discovered something wonderful.

And then I discovered that he had just discovered something wonderful. Us.

"Man, am I glad to see you guys! Hey, mind if I set up camp right here alongside you?"

Oh, if only I could be inside my dad's head to hear what he was thinking.

I couldn't resist. I knew I'd pay for it, but I just couldn't resist. Stepping closer to my dad, I said, "Hey, Dad, isn't that the..."

"Jeremiah!" My dad's volume was only a little lower than Minnesota Mike's.

I struggled not to laugh. Minnesota Mike didn't even notice. He just seemed super happy.

"I'll tell you, man." He even talked with a big smile. "I'm glad I ran into you folks, because I haven't liked camping out here by myself, doncha know, ever since I found out about the skeleton. He shows up some dark nights, they say, wandering around these parts with that lantern in his belly."

He looked up into the sky. "I don't even think there's going to be a moon out tonight. Yikes!"

CHAPTER 4

Millie

Millie sat on the floor in the living room surrounded by pictures from decades ago. She was in heaven. She'd been begging her dad for weeks to let her go through this box, ever since she discovered it in a large drawer in the garage.

Millie held up a black and white 8x10 photo of motorcycle racers standing next to their bikes. The photo was over 60 years old. Names scrawled in pencil were hard to read, but there was no doubt about the rider on the far left. Thomas Anderson. Her great grandfather. Her dad's grandfather. She never met him. He only became her great grandfather once she joined the Anderson family two years ago.

Which still wasn't a done deal, she grumbled to herself as she thought about the letter. Then her eyes wandered to the photos surrounding her. History, decades old motorcycle racing photos, that warmed her soul. She had taken to the motorcycles as if she were born with the passion to ride. Now she was a part of the fourth generation of motorcycle riders. It gave her such a sense of belonging. Finally. She had waited all her life to feel like she belonged somewhere.

She heard the phone ringing and could tell by her mom's voice it was business. It sure wasn't her dad calling to let them know how the trip was going.

She was just about to move closer to the door to eavesdrop when a newspaper clipping caught her eye. The 1897 date intrigued her, and she forgot her love of eavesdropping and focused on the headline. "Charley Arizona going to the Arctic."

What a weird thing to keep with a bunch of motorcycle pictures. She skimmed the article about this old character and his cohorts leaving the wild west to head for a new adventure in the

Arctic. Okay, so what's the big deal? Why would Great Grandpa save a hundred-year-old article with his motorcycle photos?

"First discovered by an old prospector named Charley Arizona, the eight-foot skeleton rattled around the hills for years..." Millie read, then jumped up to go show her mom.

"Ha! This is a hoot!" She headed into the next room.

"Hey, Mom!" She walked with her head down, still reading what she could make out on the weathered clipping. Her laughter died when she rounded the corner to see her mom still on the phone and sounding way too serious.

"What new development?" Her mother demanded an answer from the person on the other end. Her back was to Millie. "She's already been our daughter for two years and nothing will change that!"

Millie's heart sank. She knew that letter meant trouble.

CHAPTER 5

Jeremiah

"So Mike, I'm guessing you're from Minnesota?"

I know this trick. Dad doesn't want to listen to some harebrained story about a skeleton, so before the guy can get one more word out, he's redirecting him. I think that's something Dad learned about working with kids. Which he needs to know. Which is why we're buying the land. But I'm too focused on Minnesota Mike and the skeleton to even think about our plans.

"Well, I was from Minnesota at one point." He smiled bigger than ever. "But I ain't even been to Minnesota in years! I mean ye-e-e-e-ars!"

"Ah." Dad rubbed his ear and scratched his head. Definite signs of being annoyed. This desert trip wasn't going like we planned. I think Dad was working on another question, but Mike wasn't one to give a person long to do their part in a conversation.

"I was born and raised there and I lived there well into my adulthood, doncha know. Back when I retired, which was a little younger than most people, I decided to leave Minnesota. I'm not going back until I hit every state in the good ol' US of A at least once, maybe even twice!"

Now I saw a genuine smile cross Dad's face. So the guy wasn't sticking around? And this guy may say he retired young, but that must have been a couple decades ago. With that white beard and long white hair he could have passed for Santa. He might even be that old. Funny, he was still riding a motorcycle.

"I just decided to run down here for a quick ride. Then I'll head back west to do some surfing before I head north."

Now Dad was even happier. This guy was just planning on taking one little ride and then leaving. Maybe when he said camp with us, he just meant park with us while he went riding.

Dad rummaged through his gear bag. "Well, you take it nice and safe on your ride." Clear sign of dismissal on Dad's part.

Minnesota Mike was not catching on.

"Where did you folks want to ride to, anyway? I'm game for anywhere!"

If it weren't for the good manners my parents have been drilling into me since they met me — I know, that's a strange way to put it. But, anyway, if it weren't for those manners I would have let out the biggest, hugest, loudest, noisiest groan you ever heard.

This guy was planning on riding with us! No way! Dad had to stop this.

I needed to watch, listen and take notes. If ever I met up with a Minnesota Mike later in life, then I would know how to ditch the guy without hurting his feelings.

CHAPTER 6

Millie

Mom hit the off button but held onto the phone, staring into space.

"What did that call mean?" She jumped at the sound of Millie's voice and turned to face her.

"Millicent! What are you doing eavesdropping?"

"What did that mean? There is a problem with my adoption, isn't there? They're going to make me leave, aren't they?" Questions tumbled out of her mouth. "I knew it was too good to be true. That this would be my home. That I would finally have a real family!"

Millie stormed off toward the bathroom.

Before she could get out of the room, her mom grabbed her by the shoulders.

"Now you stop right this minute, young lady!" Surprised by how stern she sounded, Millie stopped and faced her. But the tears, those she couldn't stop.

"Millie, challenges and difficulties are a part of life." She wiped at Millie's tears with a tissue. "So none of this is surprising, but what is surprising is you reading my mail and listening in on conversations."

"It's about me! I have a right to know!"

"Later, yes. But some things are so complicated. All it does is get you worried and fearful. How does that benefit you?"

She had no response, just her sniffles while she fiddled with the newspaper clipping.

"You trust us, don't you Millie?"

She nodded.

"Then let us handle all the legal stuff involved in making this adoption final. You just worry about getting your schoolwork done and beating Jeremiah on your motorcycle." She reached out for the paper Millie was holding.

"What have you got there?"

Millie sniffed and pushed her hair out of her eyes. "This is what I was coming to show you." She held it up. "It was with the old racing photos."

"There was a light in the skeleton's rib cage according to Charley Arizona," Mom read aloud and then chuckled. "I remember this." She held the paper up and waved it in the air. "It's been years since I thought of this."

"Tell me about it, Mom!"

"I remember a silly story the family used to tell about this mysterious skeleton."

"Have you heard the whole story?" Millie's curiosity kicked into high gear.

"Well, let me give it some thought and see if I can't piece it together the way I first heard it."

"I hope you can remember the story, it's sounds exciting."

"You finish going through that box and we'll chat about it later."

CHAPTER 7

Jeremiah

So much for the note-taking, I thought later as the three of us rode east on a well-traveled dirt road called Dry Brook Highway. My dad and I had a pattern to our riding. He led, I followed and every once in a long while he hung back and let me take the lead.

We weren't sure what Minnesota Mike would do and I'm not sure he did either. He was all over that road. Sometimes in the lead and sometimes in the middle of us. Sometimes he dropped back, back, back till we thought he had taken another trail for a solo ride. Next thing you know, there'd he be again, riding alongside, nearly running into one of us.

About five miles into the ride, the gas stop and ice cream store came into view. Right next to it was the real estate office where Dad's appointment was. He was meeting a man about the property we wanted to buy. I wondered what Dad would do now, because he's always Mr. Super Secret Agent with his business. No way was he going to say anything about it with Minnesota Mike hanging around, putting his two cents worth in. Which generally ended up being more like 92 cents.

We pulled to a stop outside the store. It felt good to get my helmet off and let the breeze blow through my hair. I watched Minnesota Mike out of the corner of my eye. Wonder if Dad could ditch him here?

"Hey man, how'd you know I felt for something cold to eat?"

Dad smiled. "Well, just a hunch," he mumbled, as he smoothed down his hair and hung his helmet on the end of his handlebars.

"Say, Mike." Dad was using his best trying-to-distract-someone voice. "While you're getting ice cream, I'm going to step in the office next door and say hello to a friend."

"Hey, no problemo, man. Try to get word on that big parcel. The one that just went up for sale. That old geezer's owned it for years. I've been real interested in it myself. Maybe I'll even come along and ask the guy myself..."

"Well, I hoped you would take Jeremiah in for some ice cream too." Dad opened his fanny pack and pulled out some money.

Whew, that was close. It sounded like the land Mike was talking about, was the exact piece of property we've had our eye on.

"Yeah, okay. Besides, there's a story about gold being found on that land. Some major problem cropped up with the sale. Maybe can't even sell it now!"

Minnesota Mike stared off across the desert as if contemplating a big decision.

"You know, man, I think I'll just skip me that ice cream, save my money and see what the real scoop is on that desert land for sale." He was tossing his quarter up into the air and catching it. As if a quarter would buy anything to eat.

Dad's jaw hardened, and I saw him clenching his teeth.

A golden opportunity just presented itself and I sure wasn't going to let it pass by.

CHAPTER 8

Millie

"So what's this skeleton story all about?" Millie talked around a mouthful of pizza. "And why did he keep a newspaper clipping about it? Was he into ghost stories?"

"Don't talk with your mouth full, Millie."

"I can't help it." She still chewed and talked. "I've been waiting all day to hear the story."

"Grandpa Tom had some buddies he used to camp with..."

"In the desert where Dad and Jeremiah went?"

"I never thought about where, but I imagine it was. Your dad first went with his dad when he was a boy and maybe that's how he knew about it." Mom stopped talking while she took a bite of pizza and chewed it about a hundred times. It drove Millie crazy waiting for the rest of the story.

"They would sit around the campfire," Mom continued "and share the craziest stories. The skeleton story was the favorite."

"Were you there, Mom?"

"Oh, goodness, no. I never came along until Grandpa Tom was long gone. He handed the stories down to his son and grandson. So I heard them second and third-hand."

"Who told you?" Millie shoved another piece of pizza into her mouth.

Millie's mom frowned at the bad manners. "Was it Dad? Or did you know his dad well enough that he told you stories? How old were you, anyway, when you met Dad?"

"I was 19, and it was your dad who told me the story. We were on our way to the desert, and he was reminiscing about listening to his grandpa around the campfire."

"Wow, so Dad got to hear the ghost stories? Cool!"

"According to the legend, no one could remember where the lost desert mine was. Lost so long people doubted whether it was real. Soon people called it the Phantom Mine. The legend said the skeleton..."

The phone sang out dad's ring tone, interrupting the story.

"Ah mom, you'll be on there forever and I want to hear the story about the skeleton." Millie groaned, hoping she'd take the call later.

Her mom's face beamed when she heard her dad's voice.

"Tell me all about your trip so far." She ignored another loud groan coming from her daughter.

CHAPTER 9

Jeremiah

"Hey, Mike. I was hoping to hear more about that skeleton while we ate!"

Boy did that press the right button with old Minnesota. His face lit up and a grin the size of the Grand Canyon told me I was in for a whopper of a tale while we munched down the ice cream.

Last I saw of my dad, he was shaking his head and heading toward his appointment.

"Old Charley Arizona, was the first to spot that skeleton." Minnesota Mike jumped into the story after we got situated on a picnic bench outside. Me with an extra large milk shake while he slurped on a cone that was dripping all over his fingers. My mom would have had a cow if she could see the way he was licking his fingers.

"I hear tell he up and told people..." and at this point Mike hunched his shoulders and hunkered down. He stared me right in the eyes, his voice got lower, kinda spooky-like, as if he was Charley Arizona himself. "I could hear his old bones a'rattlin'!" Then, bam! He stood up and bellowed. "Was pert near eight, maybe even nine feet tall!"

This got embarrassing. The lady from the store rushed out to see what the commotion was. I like hearing a ghost story same as the next kid, but I didn't want to die of embarrassment in a town I hoped would soon be my hometown.

"You ain't telling that old wives tale, are ya?" She chomped on her gum while she stared at Minnesota. It popped and snapped as she waved her hand in dismissal at the crazy old man. The screen door slammed when she went back inside.

"What does she know?" Minnesota was kinda secretive like. "She must not a'heard the recent talk of gold around here."

At the mention of gold, he forgot all about telling me the scary story. "I gotta go see about that property. I mean if what they said is true about the hidden gold mine, this might be just the time to use up that old nest egg. Git me some land and settle down."

Before I could stop him, he was up and heading next door at a faster clip than I thought an old guy could go.

CHAPTER 10

Millie

"Did you make the offer?" Mom's voice sang with excitement, but legal stuff Millie didn't find interesting. She headed to the garage.

Millie had just started to clean her motorcycle when her mom showed up. She stopped what she was doing and looked up. "That was quick."

"Your dad couldn't talk, he was at the realtor's office. He wasn't able to put the offer in. There are complications."

"I don't understand any of that, but it doesn't sound good."

"When you want to buy a house, you submit an offer saying what you're willing to pay."

"Don't you just pay the price they say?" Millie squirted soapy water on the motorcycle plastics and rubbed them with a cloth while she listened.

"No, it's a little more complicated. Do you want me to explain to you how the offer works?"

"Boring!" Millie kept cleaning her bike. "Can we get back to the skeleton?"

Mom's blank stare told Millie she hadn't heard a word.

"Earth to Mom!" Millie waved her hands around, trying to get her mom's attention. "Remember the skeleton?"

"I was just thinking about the legend and your great grandpa and the property we want to buy."

"You've lost me there." Millie swung a leg over her bike and plopped down on the seat. She polished the handlebars with a different rag.

"Buying this property is a three generation dream," Mom said. "It started with your great grandpa. He loved the desert, and the tall tales, and he loved kids. He had a dream of one day starting a boys ranch."

25

"Were the boys going to ride motorcycles on this ranch?"

"Yes. Motorcycles were his passion, and he planned to use them as a rehabilitation tool for boys who'd been in trouble. But he never had the money. An amazing thing about him though. He never let go of the dream."

"How do you know that?" Millie wished she could have known him.

"After he died, the family found a notebook with handwritten notes about his plans. He dated all the pages, and he had written ideas down just a few months before he passed away."

"That's sad he never got to make his dream happen." Millie stopped polishing and found herself lost in thought like her mom, wondering about this man with the big dreams.

"His dreams kept him going." Mom nodded as she spoke. "Just because he didn't live to see it, doesn't mean his dreams won't happen."

"How could that be?"

"Like King David in the Bible." She stepped toward the door. "For all the years he planned to build the temple, he didn't get to be the one to fulfill that dream." Then, looking like she had a million things on her mind, she walked out.

Not real sure how we went from skeletons to lessons on how to sell land and then to King David, Millie thought. She probably wouldn't hear another word about the skeleton tonight.

CHAPTER 11

Jeremiah

Dad almost ran into Minnesota Mike when he came barreling out of the office next door.

"Hey there, doncha know, you're scurrying like you jist discovered gold and got to git there before the next feller!"

Dad apologized and chuckled politely. I could tell it was politely and not because he thought it was funny. He was probably tired of hearing about gold and skeletons and pretty much anything else old Minnesota had to say.

"Lunch back at camp is what I want to discover. Do you want us to wait for you?"

"No, I'm thinking I'll just hang around these parts for a while, I need to get some info from your pal here." He motioned with his thumb at the realtor's office. "You all head on back. I might catch up with you later."

I almost burst out laughing at the look of relief on my dad's face. But me, I was disappointed, because now I wouldn't get to hear the rest of the skeleton story, and why did this guy keep talking about gold?

"Mm-mmm! This is delicious!" Dad was on his second bite already of our ready-made lunch before I even got mine open. "I love your mom's sandwiches!" The fact we were eating in peace, just the two of us, made the meal even tastier. I have to admit as interesting as his stories sounded, I was also enjoying a break from our newfound friend.

Maybe when he showed back up, I'd be able to hear the rest of the story and make some sense of his ramblings about skeletons, lanterns and gold. Even if it was made up, I liked the stories.

"Push our bikes over there in the truck's shade," Dad said when I finished eating my sandwich.

"Are we going to ride over and check out our new property?" I sat back down with a cold soda and a big bag of pretzels.

"Well, Son," he sounded disappointed. "It may not become our property." He shook his head and looked at the ground. "At least not any time soon."

"What happened? I thought you went there to sign papers and give the guy some money."

"Yeah, I thought so too." Dad looked up, shaking his head again. "There are complications. The land isn't for sale."

"That makes no sense! Did someone else buy it?"

"No, he didn't say that's what happened," Dad took a long drink from his iced tea. "Your mom sure makes good iced tea!"

"What did he say about it being for sale two weeks ago?"

"Said he jumped the gun putting the for sale sign up. He doesn't have a signed contract yet."

"Oh." I was disappointed but still hopeful. "Well, at least it didn't get sold to someone else."

"Yeah. If that's really the story."

Uh-oh. That didn't sound good.

"What do you mean?" I jumped up in frustration, knocking over my drink and spilling the pretzels. Which was okay because pretzels weren't my favorite. I wanted Flamin' Hot Cheetos, but my mom didn't pack those.

"I just feel like something is up, but I can't put my finger on it." Dad stared across the desert.

"That's not fair!" I yelled. "What about all our plans? What about our kids ranch? What about me riding my motorcycle every day? It isn't fair!"

I knocked over the lawn chair and kicked my soda can. "We might as well go home, at least everything is okay there."

Dad picked up my lawn chair and the soda can and even the pretzel bag. "Well, not everything."

CHAPTER 12

Millie

"Hey, Mom!" Millie ran into the house searching for her. "Hey, Mom!" she called out again just as she rounded the corner into her mom's office.

"Millie! You scared me!" Mom clutched her chest. "Is something wrong?"

"No, I just had this great idea!"

Mom took her glasses off and rubbed her eyes. It looked like she had been staring at her laptop. Millie stepped around the desk to see what was so interesting. As usual, Mom had a bazillion tabs open on her browser. She clicked out of them when Millie got to where she could see the screen.

Forgetting what she came running in for, Millie's curiosity grew, knowing her mom was looking up something she didn't want her to see.

"What were you studying?"

Mom waved her hand in the air as if to dismiss her research as nothing of importance. "Oh, you know how I get Millie, just following a rabbit trail through the internet. Jumping from one thing to the next."

"But why did you click from the browser to your email as soon as I stepped around?"

"Oh Millie, really!" she put her glasses back on and snapped her laptop shut. "You know how far behind I get on my emails."

"Yeah, but you only got interested in your email when I came around to this side of your desk."

"Millie, you sound like a detective on a hot lead." Mom laughed and reached over to hug her. "So what did you want when you came running in, practically scaring me to death?" A forced laugh. Millie could tell.

"Maybe I am a detective." She refused to give up. "I know you didn't decide to answer emails at the exact moment I came in. I know you're reading about stuff you're hiding from me. Probably something about that letter or phone call. What was that phone call about?"

"Millie, please..."

"You keep saying that! Stop saying that!" Her voice rose louder than she meant.

Mom stared right at her. "Honestly!" She opened the laptop and clicked the mouse on one of the open tabs. Millie noticed it wasn't the last tab she was on and was just about to ask her why she didn't click on the one she was hiding until she caught sight of the topic.

"Legend of the skeleton in the desert!"

"Does that look like secret social worker research?"

"Oh." Now she forced a laugh. "I thought you were keeping something from me. Something bad."

Now Mom's laugh was genuine. "Maybe I was keeping something from you. I didn't want you to know I was curious about that silly old legend about the skeleton!"

While they laughed together, Mom closed the laptop. "What did you come running in for?"

"Oh yeah," Millie pushed her hair behind her ears and plopped down on the edge of Mom's desk. "I had the most awesome idea. Can I read the notebook Great Grandpa had about the boys ranch idea? Do you think Dad would let me read the journal?"

Mom's smile vanished. "That is a sad memory for your dad."

"Why?"

"Because the journal burned in a fire."

"Fire? Did someone's house burn down?"

"No. Someone threw it into a fire."

"Who would do that?"

"Millie, I'm sorry, but I can't talk about that without asking your dad. I shouldn't have mentioned the journal."

"But Mom! You can't leave me just hanging like this! First the skeleton story you haven't finished and now a mystery that involves my own family. Pleeease!!"

She could tell by the look on her mom's face no amount of begging would help. She wished she could get onto her mom's laptop to check the browsing history. Millie knew her mom was hiding more than the skeleton website.

CHAPTER 13

Jeremiah

"What do you mean everything isn't okay at home?"

Wouldn't you know it? Right when I needed to have a serious conversation with my dad, out of nowhere a motorcycle comes roaring in and slides to a stop in a cloud of dust.

"Hey there, hey now!" Minnesota Mike ripped his helmet off so fast it looked like his head would come off with it.

"What's happening here? You're not loading up and heading home, are you? You're not leaving, are you?"

Wow, this guy could talk. It was hard to get a word in.

"We've had a change in plans." Dad packed his jersey and riding pants into his gear bag.

"Doncha know, I got some news for you!" Minnesota popped open a soda can. "Let me down this pop first, I'm dying of thirst." He guzzled the soft drink we call soda. Dad kept packing, but Minnesota Mike just wasn't having it.

"Hey now, you gotta hear what I have to say and I think you'll change your mind about leaving." He followed that with a loud burp that would have sent my mom into orbit. "Whew! That hit the spot!" He patted his protruding stomach. Not sure the guy's heard of manners. But it was pretty funny. It almost made me forget about whatever was going on at home. Almost, but not quite.

"Come on, guys. Pull up a chair." He pulled his out of the back of his pickup truck. "You gotta hear what I learnt about that property for sale."

I saw Dad look at him. But I know how my dad thinks. He won't want this guy to think he's interested or to know how important that property is to us.

"I could use a rest and a cold drink before we hit the road."

Okay, now I knew for sure my dad wanted to hear what Minnesota Mike had to say. We had both just finished eating lunch and Dad just downed a big glass of iced tea.

"What's your hurry to git out of this place? Ya looked like you were all set to stay a few days."

Dad ignored the question and dropped into a chair with a cold water. I grabbed a bottle too and sat next to him.

"I never tip my hand what I know about things," Minnesota Mike said, "but I just wandered in all nonchalant-like and asked the guy what properties did he have for sale. He talked about every property this side of the moon but never mentioned THE property. You know, the big parcel that's got my interest and maybe yours, too."

How did he know that? I wondered. We didn't say anything about it.

"Least wise," Minnesota Mike continued, "that's what the guy in the office said when I told him the parcel that got my interest."

"What's that?" Dad's ears perked up when he realized the realtor was talking about him.

"Yeah, the guy said it was strange he'd get two people right in a row asking about the same parcel of land that ain't even for sale."

"What parcel is that?" I never knew Dad was so good at acting like he didn't know stuff. It's not actually lying, but it sure isn't admitting the truth.

Minnesota looked at him kinda strange, maybe wondering why Dad pretended he didn't just ask that guy about the land. Then he went back to his rambling.

"It's the gold! I know it's the gold. That's why..."

"Why do you keep talking about gold?" I interrupted. Dad gave me a look for butting in, but I think he was as curious as I was.

"Sure! The word is out there's gold on that land and now they're rethinking selling."

"Why do you think there's gold on land for sale out here?" Dad still didn't admit he knew what land it was.

Minnesota looked a little ashamed. "Well, I'll tell ya." He stared into the sky, then got up and took another can out of the ice chest in his truck. He popped it open, but just sipped on it. I don't even think he was thirsty, it's like he was stalling. Trying to decide what to tell us.

Dad was patient. I was not. But I didn't push my luck and ask. I just kept staring at him, waiting for the answer.

"Yeah, I'll tell ya." He was still looking up in the sky, then around the desert. Then back at my dad. "I'm not real proud about this, but there's a reason I know about the gold."

It seemed like he would never tell us.

He sat back down in his chair and stared at the ground for so long it was like he had forgotten what we were talking about. Forgot about his soda too. It tipped over in the dirt and the brown liquid oozing out made a mud puddle around the can.

Dad was growing impatient. He stood up and crushed his empty water bottle. "Sounds like nothing more than a legend." Dad returned to packing.

"I admit," Minnesota came to life. "It sounds far-fetched, but I got it on good authority."

Dad turned to look at him again, and me, well, I never stopped looking at him. I wanted to shake the story out of him, but I was too polite.

"Tell ya what though." Minnesota Mike stood and rubbed his chin. "You're good folks and I... Well, I just can't bring myself to tell ya how I know."

CHAPTER 14

Millie

Millie crept down the hallway and listened outside her mom's door. She could hear the shower water, so she hurried to the office.

Lifting the laptop open, her heart beat hard as she touched the mouse to bring the screen to life. She had to see what her mom was hiding. But she was taking a big risk. Both she and Jeremiah knew their mom's work laptop was off limits.

Clicking through the open tabs, she stopped when she saw a website about birth parents and adoption. She knew it was something about her adoption. Before skimming through the huge amount of text, she clicked another tab and saw a public records search for someone named Boyd Colston. Who was Boyd Colston? Why would Mom be researching him? That sure wasn't her biological dad's name. Maybe he was a new client.

That didn't seem likely as she read over the results of the public records search. Quite a criminal history this Boyd character had. Did not sound like someone who would hire a virtual assistant like Mom.

Mom had paid for the background info, so whoever this character was, he was worth $59.95 for her to learn about.

Millie jumped at the sound of her Mom's bedroom door opening. Breathing fast and with a pounding heart, she clicked back to the email and shut the laptop.

"Millie?" The voice floated down the hall.

She jumped out of the office chair and hurried to the hallway. "Did you need me Mom?"

The door cracked open a few inches. She saw her mom's dripping wet hair and part of her face.

"Yes, I'm sure you know why!" She didn't sound happy.

How could she have known? Millie wondered. Did she have secret cameras at her desk? Was her web cam synced with her phone? "I'm dead!" Millie moaned to herself.

"My conditioner!" Mom sounded annoyed.

Millie wanted to laugh out loud with relief but she knew that was the wrong response.

"I'm sorry Mom! I'm so sorry." She ran to the bathroom she and Jeremiah shared, grabbed her Mom's hair conditioner and hurried back down the hall with it.

Before her Mom could say anything else, she blurted out, "I know you've told me a hundred times not to take it without permission. I'm so sorry I inconvenienced you."

Mom was silent. Did she go overboard on that apology? Millie wondered. She wanted to get on her mom's good side. The guilt for touching the laptop was overwhelming.

"Thank you." Mom closed the bedroom door and Millie realized she still had a little more time.

Standing in the office doorway, she knew there were answers waiting there for her. If only she dared take another look.

She had to know what was going on. But what if she got caught? Would it be worth it?

CHAPTER 15

Jeremiah

That was all it took. My dad was done listening to Minnesota Mike's ramblings about skeletons and property for sale and gold. He worked faster than ever cleaning up the area and moving the bikes in place to load into the truck.

"Now wait jist a minute. You folks aren't leaving, are you?" Minnesota Mike was whining now. "Thought you was staying all night, doncha know?"

"We thought about it," Dad didn't look at Minnesota, but moved even faster, if that was possible. The tailgate dropped open with a loud thump, very unlike Dad. He was super careful with all his stuff. I guess between running into this guy, getting the bad news about the property and now bad news from home, it was all too much.

"Well?" Minnesota prompted. "Ya sure didn't consider it for long then?"

"Something came up at home." Dad's voice sounded strained as he pushed his bike up the ramp onto the tailgate. I was so stunned at what was taking place I had forgotten to help push. But the look he gave - that look that says I'm going to die if I don't get over there and help him - lit a fire under me. Soon we had his bike in the truck bed. I hurried to the side and handed him the tie straps to cinch it down.

Then, because it was just that kind of day where you need nothing else to go wrong, I hurried over to my bike and rolled it to the edge of the ramp.

"Well, I'm right disappointed." Minnesota Mike's head hung down. You'd think we were old friends. "I was hoping to jaw with you about that property we're both so interested in."

"Look!" Dad's voice raised. "Why do you keep saying we're both interested in that property?"

36

"Well that feller, the real estate guy, told me you were asking about it."

"Well, so what if I was?" Dad said, as we pushed my bike up the ramp.

"It's because I wouldn't tell you how I knowed about the gold, ain't it? That's why you're leaving!"

Dad stopped so fast the bike rolled back down the ramp a few inches. I held on to it in mid-climb while he stared down Minnesota. "I don't mean to be rude here, Mike, but you're trying my patience and I've had about enough of your talk about gold and skeletons and properties for sale."

"Well now..." Minnesota Mike said.

"You don't need to fill my boy's head full of ghost stories and frankly, I've had some bad news from home and just need to get loaded up and hit the road."

Next thing I knew, Minnesota was behind my bike helping push it so Dad could pull it up into the truck bed where he was standing. "Man, am I sorry to hear that. I'll help any way I can. You won't hear no more of me going on about all I've discovered, when you got more important things on your mind."

He didn't seem offended. He also didn't seem to let go of the idea he had valuable info we might want to know.

Within minutes, we were back out on the two-lane highway heading west, chasing the sun that would soon dip past the mountains we had to cross. It was almost dusk when I saw the strangest thing in the distance.

Maybe I'd heard too much about the skeleton today, but there was something weird hovering just above the ground. I blinked my eyes and turned my head farther to my left, trying to see around my dad's head.

It couldn't be? Or could it? It sure is tall enough to be the skeleton Minnesota Mike had been rambling about. But it looks more like a ghost. Not that I've ever seen a ghost.

I shook my head and looked again. Nothing there. Even turning around and looking out the back window, I couldn't see it.

"Son, what on earth are you doing?"

"Oh, heh, heh." Wow, even I thought my laugh sounded phony. "Just saying goodbye to the desert I thought I was camping in tonight."

"Well, turn back around. You're distracting me with all that moving around."

Dad definitely had something on his mind. I knew he was as disappointed as I was about not getting the property deal started. That was the whole reason we had come out today.

"Dad, what's the bad news from home?"

I don't think he even heard me. He gets like that sometimes. Like he's lost in his own mind, concentrating on things so hard he doesn't know anyone is talking to him.

"Dad!" He looked my way, then back at the highway. I found that always works. Get his attention first, then ask.

"What's the bad news from home?"

"Oh that." He chuckled. Was that a pretend chuckle? "I just said the first thing I could think of to get him to stop pestering me."

"But before he pulled up, you said something was wrong at home."

"I did?" He stared at the road. He was a bad liar. Not enough practice, I guess.

"Yes, you did!"

"Oh, I don't even remember now. That guy has me so frustrated, I can't think."

Sure. Secrets in the desert. Secrets at home. What was going on?

CHAPTER 16

Millie

"Yes," Millie whispered. It would be worth it, even if she got caught.

She sat down in her mom's chair and opened the laptop again, clicking to the third tab from the left.

"Summary of criminal charges," the heading read. She scanned the list. Identity theft, robbery, fraud.

Millie tensed as she heard the faint chirping of her mom's phone. Maybe if she got into a long conversation, this would give her more time. The phone continued to chirp. Her mom must still be in the shower. Silence.

She couldn't waste any more time. The list went on. Boyd must have been a career criminal. There was something about dishonorable discharge from military service, whatever that meant. Still not what she was looking for.

The phone was chirping again. The ringtone wasn't familiar. "Hello?" She could hear the muffled sound of her mom taking the call. "Yes, this is Norah Anderson."

She was out of the shower. Not much time left.

Millie stared back at the screen, scrolling to page two of the criminal summary. At the top was a new heading. This was the one she was expecting to see.

"Child Protective Services," she whispered. Bingo! This was the information she needed to find out what was going on in her life. Single space typing with scattered black marks across the page hid random words. Names of children, she guessed.

"Millie!" the voice carried down the hall. She hadn't even heard the bedroom door open.

"Yeah, Mom?" Millie yelled to cover the sound of the laptop clicking shut. She jumped out of the chair and ran to her mom's bedroom. Thankfully, her mom was just peeking out the door again.

"Millie! You will not believe it! It's so wonderful!" Mom squealed.

Millie shook from the close call. She did her best to sound interested, but her mind was back on the browser and the secrets it held.

"What's up, Mom?" She took a deep breath to stop the quiver in her voice.

"Pack your bags! We're going to the desert!"

This made no sense. "Are we driving out to meet Dad?"

"No!" Mom was laughing. This was getting weirder. "Hold on! I need to get dressed and I'll tell you all about it. But get your bag packed! I'll be right out."

Millie sat in the middle of her room staring at the overnight bag. The words "Child Protective Services" floated in front of her. The bag was still empty when Mom rushed through the door minutes later.

"It's so wonderful, your dad will be thrilled." She didn't even notice Millie hadn't packed a thing. "That was the realtor on the phone, the property is for sale!" Mom clapped her hands. "Your Dad just won't believe it. It was a mix-up on the parcel numbers in the system. There is another man interested, but he's giving us first chance if we can get back there tonight."

"You mean the dream still might happen?" She jumped up and embraced her mom, who noticed the empty bag.

"Yes, now come on goofball, you gotta get packing. Your dad will be home soon and I want to be ready! This time we're going with him."

"What do you mean, Dad won't believe it? Doesn't he know?"

"He sure doesn't." Mom floated out of the room on a cloud. "The man couldn't get a hold of him. Lots of dead areas on the drive home."

She could hear her mom going through drawers in the next room as she packed her own bag.

"But why was he driving home? They were supposed to stay the night!" She followed her mom into her bedroom.

"Oh Millie, so many questions!" Mom said. "They changed their plans. Now pack, girl! They'll be here soon."

CHAPTER 17

Jeremiah

The only thing I wanted to do when we got home was eat, shower and hit the sack. This had been a long disappointing day. I looked over at Dad and could tell he felt the same way.

Making the last turn onto our street, I couldn't believe my eyes. My mom and sister were out on the front porch. It looked like every light in the house was on. What was going on?

"What in the world?" Dad said.

He pulled into the driveway and Mom and Millie ran out and surrounded us when we stepped out of the truck.

"We're getting the property!" Millie told the entire neighborhood.

Mom shushed her, but then let out her own shriek at the surprised look on Dad's face. "It's true, Max!" she jumped up and down. This couldn't be my mom, could it?

Dad came to life and threw his arms around Mom. Then stepped back, looking into her face. "But how? Why?"

Mom tugged on both of us to come inside, "Hurry, we have to get ready to head back!"

She set out leftovers from last night's dinner and filled us in on the details while we ate.

This was unbelievably great. Just when I lost all hope, we come home and find hope waiting for us.

"I don't know who or what he's talking about," Mom said as we were finishing our food. "But he said some other guy wants the property too."

I groaned. "Oh no, he does want it!"

"Who? Who!" Millie sounded like a barn owl.

"Some crazy guy we met down in the desert, calls himself Minnesota Mike."

Mom looked at Dad.

He chuckled and nodded his head. "Yes, Norah, I'm afraid it's true. It's been quite a day."

"Well, let's quit talking and get on the road," Millie urged.

Mom and Millie had the SUV loaded with their overnight bags. We took ours out of the truck and put them in the back of the car with theirs. Dad pulled the truck into the garage so we didn't have to take time to unload our bikes.

"Next time we'll have the trailer and all the bikes. We'll make it a celebration trip for a week!" Dad said as he backed out of the driveway.

"What's the story on this Minnesota Mike character?" Mom looked over at Dad as he pulled onto the freeway and hit the cruise control.

"Just some nutty guy." Dad took a long drink of the iced tea Mom brought along for him.

"Yeah," I chimed in, "just some nutty guy talking about gold and skeletons and..."

"Skeletons!" Millie shouted.

"Yes, skeletons. What's the big deal?" I said, as if we talked about skeletons every day.

"We've been talking about skeleton stories around here today, too!"

"Are you kidding me?"

"No, you can ask Mom."

Before I could get my question out Mom turned to look at her. "Not now, Millie."

She wasn't easily discouraged once she got an idea into her head. She didn't look like she was going to accept Mom putting the conversation off.

"Is that the bad news that happened around here today?" I jumped in before Millie could stay on the skeleton subject.

Mom looked over at Dad. "You told him?"

I could see Dad looking at me in the mirror. Guess I shouldn't have opened my mouth. Before I could wonder any more about what was going on, Millie spoke up.

"No, the skeleton wasn't the bad news." She did not look happy. "Boyd Colston was!"

Mom's head turned toward the back seat so fast it scared me. By the look on Millie's face she knew she had said something she shouldn't have.

"Where did you hear that name?" Mom demanded.

CHAPTER 18

Millie

Millie froze as her mom glared at her.

"Millicent! I asked you a question!"

Millie hated that name. "I don't know!" she yelled. She could see Jeremiah looking stunned. Yelling at parents was a big no-no in this family.

Her dad glanced at her in the mirror.

"You didn't just pull that name out of thin air." Mom stared without blinking. "I'm waiting."

Millie sat in silence, turning her head to stare out the side window.

"Millie," her dad's voice was quiet. "Answer your mother."

She hated it when he talked like that. It was much easier for parents to yell, because then you could just yell back and figure they deserved it.

"I don't know," she repeated, this time in a softer voice. Then she shrugged. "I heard you say it today."

Mom wasn't buying it. "No, I did not mention that name today."

"Sure you did, when you were on the phone talking and I walked in." It sounded convincing to her, but still no sale.

"You were on my laptop, weren't you?"

The car slowed and the loud click-click of the blinker echoed in the silence. Her mom turned to see what Dad was doing.

"Max?"

"We need a little break." He pulled onto the off ramp that led to a traveler's rest stop.

The car rolled to a stop under a bright street light, far away from the 18-wheeled trucks parked at the other end of the lot.

Dad motioned Mom to get out of the car. Before her door clicked shut Millie heard her angry words. "Max, you know the kids aren't allowed to touch my laptop."

Dad put his arm around her and they walked away from the car.

"I can't believe you did that!" Jeremiah whispered.

"Did what?" Millie squeaked out as tears fell.

"You know what. You used Mom's laptop. Otherwise you wouldn't have given her such lame answers."

"So what if I did?"

"Who is the guy, anyway?"

"I don't know! But I think it has something to do with why my adoption is dragging out. How long did it take for your adoption to be completed?"

"I don't know, Millie! I never paid attention to that. I was their son from the day I moved in. That's all I know."

"Oh, come on, Jeremiah!" Millie wiped her tears on the bottom of her shirt. "You know it's not safe until the adoption is final. I also know yours didn't take as long as mine."

"So, what if it is taking longer?"

"It's because something is going wrong with my adoption. I think it has something to do with that Boyd dude."

Millie saw her parents heading back to the car. Now she would get it. They had time to plot together and figure out what awful punishment they figured she deserved.

The door opened and her parents got back in.

"You know what we forgot to do before we left home?" Dad said. No one responded.

"We forgot to pray." He took his hat off and reached out for her mom's hand. Mom turned in her seat, but this time instead of looking angry, she smiled at Millie and took her hand.

Millie could feel tears begin again. Now her nose was running too, as she listened to the soothing sound of her Dad's voice, talking to God about their trip, asking Him to bless their plans. He asked for safety as they traveled and for renewed joy in their family.

"And God, protect our daughter Millie and please finish up her adoption soon! Amen."

The tears fell faster than ever now. Right when she thought she was in big trouble, they're praying for her. Who could figure out parents? Especially these parents. Mom dug around in her purse and handed a tissue back to Millie. She smiled and winked at her.

Dad pulled the car back onto the highway. As he got up to

speed in the darkness, he glanced in the mirror again, a sparkle in his eye.

"Say," he looked over at Jeremiah, too. "Did I ever tell you kids about the desert skeleton story my grandpa used to tell me?"

CHAPTER 19

Jeremiah

"Are you kidding me, Dad? Now you're sounding like Minnesota Mike!"

Dad glanced at me in the mirror. He was in a much better frame of mind tonight. Earlier in the day there was nothing about old Minnesota that would have made Dad laugh.

"Yes, I guess I kind of do," he admitted, chuckling.

"Who is this Minnesota Mike guy?" Millie asked.

"Yes, I'd like to know too." Mom looked at Dad.

"Well, make up your minds. I can't tell two stories at once. What'll it be, Minnesota Mike or the skeleton in the desert?"

The car filled with loud chatter as we all gave our opinions. We settled on our friend in the desert, saving the skeleton story for later.

"Where to start?" Dad sounded like we had known the guy a hundred years.

"Let me start, Dad!" I jumped in. I loved a good story, and I knew I'd tell it more colorfully than Dad.

"It all started when this idiot," and I emphasized the word idiot, "blew by us on that little winding desert highway..."

"Jeremiah! That wasn't necessary."

"No, but it sure was fun!"

After the laughter died down, we filled Mom and Millie in on everything the two of us could remember about Minnesota Mike.

"I wonder if we'll ever see him again?" I said.

"Hopefully not in this lifetime!" Dad smiled at me in the mirror.

"Aw, he wasn't that bad."

"No, that's just why it took the whole drive to the desert to cover everything about our day with him," Dad said.

"I can't believe we're almost there," Mom said. "That was quite a story to pass the time." She reached into the small cooler at her feet and popped open a diet soda can. "Anyone want something to drink?"

"Do you think he was right about the gold story?" Millie honed in on the most intriguing part, not even hearing Mom's question. "Do you think he was talking about our property?"

"It sounded like he knew what he was talking about," I said.

"Now Jeremiah, he didn't sound like he knew what he was talking about regarding anything he said."

"Well, he knew about the property for sale, didn't he?"

"That's a no-brainer. There are for sale signs scattered throughout the desert.

"He knew you were interested in the property." I wasn't ready to give up on the idea that there was some truth to the gold story.

"I wasn't too happy with that realtor tipping him off that I was interested. That should have been private. Most likely the guy was using it to generate interest in the parcel."

"Why would he do that, though, if he was saying it wasn't for sale?"

"Is that what the guy told you, Dad?" Millie said. "Did he tell you right to your face the property wasn't for sale?"

"Yes and it was disappointing hearing it. But like he told your Mom, it was a mix-up with the parcel numbers."

"Maybe it was and maybe it wasn't." My mind churned out a dozen mysterious scenarios.

"What do you mean by that, Jeremiah?" Mom looked over her shoulder at me.

"Well, maybe it's true there is gold on the property and the realtor man wants to buy it himself. So he just tells anyone who asks that it isn't for sale anymore. How about that?"

"Yeah." Millie got caught up in the story line. "And maybe later in the day he learned that the gold is on the property next door to ours and decided he could sell it after all."

"You kids read too many mysteries," Dad said.

Millie wasn't giving up. "Did Minnesota Mike say how he knew about the gold?"

"He said someone told him. Isn't that right, Dad?"

"He was vague about it." Dad slowed the car while clicking on his blinker. "He said he had it on good authority, but he wouldn't tell us more." He pulled the car up next to the realtor's office. Bright lights shone through the windows. The gas station and ice cream store were dark.

"I remember now!" I wasn't ready to get out till we convinced Dad there might be gold. "He said we were good folks, and that's why he didn't want to tell us how he knew."

Mom was looking in the visor mirror, brushing her hair and putting gunk on her lips. "Sounds like he's just making excuses for his made-up story." She looked at Dad. "Ready to go sign up for the next adventure in our lives?" She had the biggest smile as she grabbed the door handle.

Dad and Mom were greeting the guy by the time we got out of the car. He stood on the porch motioning for us to come in.

Just before I stepped up onto the weather beaten wood planks, Millie grabbed my arm.

"Jeremiah!" she screeched. "Look over there!"

CHAPTER 20

Millie

"It's the skeleton!" Millie took off running into the darkness before Jeremiah could respond.

Off in the distance she saw a ghostly-looking figure floating above the ground. She couldn't make it out for sure, but it looked a lot like a giant skeleton. Coming from inside him, or wait, maybe it was at his side, a dim light. "It's the lantern! Just like the legend!"

"Millie, come back here!" Jeremiah ran to catch up with her.

She ignored him and kept going, "It's the skeleton! I know it!" She turned back to look at Jeremiah, but lost her footing and fell onto the asphalt. She put out her hands and saved herself from a face plant into the black gravel. Dad taught her to do that when she first started riding motorcycles and was crashing so much. Jeremiah caught up to her as she scrambled to get up. She looked back at the skeleton, but it had disappeared over the ridge.

"It was him!" she yelled into Jeremiah's face as he took hold of her shoulders and tried to quiet her.

"Stop! Mom and Dad will hear you and think we're crazy."

"I know I saw him, didn't you see him, Jeremiah? You were right behind me!"

"No, I didn't." He helped her brush the gravel off her knees. "Well, I don't think I did." He hesitated. "Maybe I did see something, but I couldn't say it was a skeleton."

"Well, it sure wasn't human." Millie was insistent. "It was floating in the air."

"I don't know, Millie." Jeremiah shook his head.

"You saw something." She stared into his eyes. "It sure wasn't walking on land, was it?"

"I was too busy staring at my lame brain sister. I knew you would fall the way you were charging ahead."

They both breathed hard as they headed back to the office.

"Well, at least we know Minnesota Mike isn't crazy."

"Ha!" Jeremiah howled. "More like, you're just as crazy as he is." He laughed as they made their way over to the lighted parking area. But Millie noticed his laugh was stilted. She wondered why. He probably saw it, but didn't want to encourage her. He was too level-headed to believe something like that existed. Even with the evidence right in front of them.

They were almost to the building when Millie grabbed his arm again.

"Jeremiah!" she screeched. "Look over there! He's back!"

CHAPTER 21

Jeremiah

That girl scared me half to death. She gripped my arm so tight with one hand I thought her nails would dig into my skin right through my jacket. She pointed into the darkness.

I could see movement at the other end of the parking lot and a faint flicker of light.

"It's him, Jeremiah! It's the skeleton with the lantern. I told you I saw him!" She was still screeching, but now it was a whispery weird kind of screech, like someone losing their voice.

I could see Mom and Dad sitting in the office and they seemed to have forgotten about us. I figured it was okay to investigate before we went in.

As I took a few steps toward the creature, Millie grabbed the back of my jacket. "No! It's not safe!"

"Well, you weren't scared before." I tried to yank my jacket away from her.

"He wasn't coming in our direction before!"

The outline of a man took shape. He was heading toward us, swinging a lantern.

"Millie, you have skeletons on the brain. That's just a man. Look! Skin, clothes, hair. I don't see any bones sticking out, do you?"

"Why is he wandering around in the dark?" She was so jumpy.

"I don't know, maybe he lives here."

As he got closer, we could see a white beard and wispy hair sticking out under a beanie cap. "Hey, that must be your M&M guy!" she whispered in my ear, still hanging onto my jacket.

"M&M guy? What are you talking about?"

"You know, that mountain man or mountain Mike or whatever you called him." She stared across the parking lot.

I almost laughed out loud. "Minnesota Mike, and that is way easier to say." I stepped up on the porch. "Yeah, I like that!"

"Where are you going?"

"Inside, to hear what's going on." I opened the door and turned back to her. "And no, that's not our M&M guy."

"Oh." Millie sounded disappointed we hadn't discovered the living breathing skeleton legend and not even M&M.

"There you are!" Mom looked up as we walked into the office, shielding our eyes, as they adjusted to the bright light. "What were you doing out there?"

"Just watching a guy across the parking lot," I said.

"That's Gus, my maintenance man," Mr. Property Seller Guy said, without looking up from the paperwork he had spread across his desk. "He likes to take a walk by lantern light every evening before bed."

"Oh, I thought it was the..."

I jumped in before Millie could mention the skeleton. "He startled us. We thought we were the only crazy people out here at this time of night." I laughed like I had just made a big joke. The adults ignored us and continued signing thousands of pieces of paper. Or maybe not quite that many.

Millie shot me a dirty look for interrupting and I shot her one back for being stupid enough to mention the skeleton legend in front of this guy.

It seemed they would never be done signing papers. I looked over and saw Millie studying a brochure on the table next to where she was sitting.

"What's that?" I said, as I sat in the chair next to her.

She held it up. "The History of Dry Brook," I read. "Hey, that looks interesting."

"You kids are welcome to take one of those."

I looked over at the realtor.

"I have lots of those." He reached into his desk drawer and pulled out a stack of brochures. "They didn't prove to be as popular as I thought. You can each take one."

"Amos, thank you very much for letting us come down this late." Dad stood up to leave several minutes later.

"I'll call you as soon as we get a response from the seller."

I stared at the guy, listening to the sound of his voice, trying to decide if he was honest. What was going on with this property? I wasn't sure I believed the story about the gold discovery. I didn't know much. In fact, nothing, about buying land. But something did not seem right. The property was for sale, then it wasn't for sale, then it was for sale.

"Who was the other guy who wanted to buy it?" I asked, remembering what Mom told us back at the house.

"Jeremiah," Dad scolded. "That isn't appropriate for you to ask."

Amos chuckled. "It's all right, Mr. Anderson. I remember what it was like to be a curious youngster." He turned in my direction. "An older gentleman. Not from around here. He came in after your dad did. Had a strange name."

He looked back at Dad and Mom. "But you had inquired first, so I wanted to give you first crack at it."

"Minnesota Mike?" Everyone looked at Millie. Mom's eyes said volumes as she stared at her but she didn't speak.

"Yes, young lady. That was his name. He said he would be camping in the area and was eager to put in an offer."

"Well, we appreciate you giving us first chance," Mom said. "How long before we'll have an answer from the seller?"

"Oh, didn't I tell you?" Before Amos could tell us whatever it was he forgot to tell us, his phone rang. He looked down at the caller ID. "I'm sorry. I need to get this." He shook my dad's hand, signaling the end of the unfinished conversation.

CHAPTER 22

Millie

Millie noticed a car speeding toward them as they pulled out of the parking lot, seconds before impact, not in enough time to warn her dad.

The car hit the front driver's side of the SUV with such force they spun around facing back into the parking lot they had just pulled out of. Millie's body jerked forward, but the seatbelt held her rigid, biting into her neck. The harsh sound of metal on metal echoed in her ears. A man's grinning face staring at them, before he sped off into the night, embedded itself in her mind.

"Keep your belts on," Dad said. He spun the steering wheel around, giving the car so much gas the wheels screeched on the pavement. "We'll catch that guy!"

"Max, slow down!" Mom said.

A quarter mile away, the front tire blew, and they skidded to a stop.

"Drat!" Dad slammed both hands on the steering wheel. "I wanted his license plate number."

"Dad!" Millie sobbed. "That man swerved for us!"

"He sure did, Dad, he came in our lane on purpose."

Millie looked out the window and saw Gus the maintenance man running along the highway, his lantern swinging at his side.

Dad didn't respond to them, just punched 911 into his phone. "Need to report a hit and run."

Millie and Jeremiah hopped out of the car as Gus reached them. Mom joined them, putting her arm around Millie, hugging her to her side. "Thank God, we're okay."

The broken driver's side headlight left a trail of scattered glass on the asphalt road. Steam spewed out of the radiator where the grill pushed through it.

"I've got 911 on the line!" Amos, the realtor man, shouted as he caught up to the group.

"My dad's talking with them now," Jeremiah said.

Millie's teeth chattered. She couldn't get a single word out, when her mom asked if she was okay. She nodded and swiped at tears.

"Your dad must not have seen him, when he pulled out," Amos said.

"That guy aimed for us!" Millie blurted out. The minute he implied her dad might have been at fault, she forgot she was cold and scared. "He laughed when he hit us!" She stared at the realtor, as if he caused the crash.

"Millie, Millie. It's okay." Her mom led her to the other side of the car where her dad stood outside the door.

"I meant nothing by it, Mrs. Anderson."

"Yeah, sure!" Millie said under her breath. Her mom squeezed her tight.

"Did you see the accident happen, Gus?" Jeremiah discussed the wreck with the maintenance man on the other side of the SUV, but she wanted to listen to her dad.

"What did they say, Max?"

"They took the information, but won't send anyone out tonight, since no one is hurt. There's only one deputy on duty so we'll hear from him tomorrow."

"Good! I have something to tell him. I think Mr. Know-Everything Realtor Guy caused this."

Mom looked stunned. "Millie! What makes you think he's involved?" Dad looked as if he also wanted an answer.

"When you went to the car, I ran back into his office because I left my jacket on the chair."

Dad looked at her. "And?"

"It's what I overheard while he was on the phone." She looked at her dad. "I'm sure he's involved!"

CHAPTER 23

Jeremiah

The tow truck arrived as I was trying to break away from Gus. It sounded like Millie's conversation was way more interesting.

I was too late for the good stuff.

"We'll discuss this later." Dad motioned us to move away from the highway as the tow truck maneuvered into place. The reality of our wrecked car hit me. What are we supposed to do now? Hang out with Gus and Amos? Maybe even a skeleton?

It seemed like ages ago we were having fun talking about a silly ghost story. Now we were stuck in the desert with a not-so-honest salesman, a maintenance man who was a dead ringer for M&M and who knew what other weird creatures. My stomach growled, and I was cold and tired, too.

"Jeremiah!" Dad's voice penetrated my foggy brain. I don't know how many times he called me. No wonder he kept getting louder and louder.

I hurried over in his direction.

"Get our bags from the back. Millie!" He turned his attention away from me. "Check the back seat for jackets, backpacks and anything else. Grab whatever you find."

Mom rifled through the front seat, gathering things she and Dad brought.

"Do you need me to give you a lift anywhere?" Amos called out to Dad. "I can drive you anywhere you need to go."

"Yeah, you should be helping." Millie muttered as I slammed the back doors shut. I set the bags where Dad told me and hurried over to the side door.

"What's that about, Millie? Why are you mad at the realtor?"

She glanced over her shoulder before answering. "He told the person on the phone, 'they're leaving now, they'll be pulling out any minute.'"

She stared right into my eyes, her own eyes as big as a giant squid's. "So there! What does that mean? Kinda strange, not long after I overhear his comment, a car comes out of nowhere and crashes into us."

Before I answered, Dad said, "Hurry, you two. Get clear of the car. He's ready to load it."

Dad sat up front with the driver and the three of us had plenty of room in the large backseat compartment. Millie obsessed over our wrecked car out the back window, while I, on the other hand, stared in awe at the digital map and radios mounted to the dash. The large roadmap glowed an eerie green in the dark night and a red blip of a light blinked our course along the highway.

Thirty minutes later the tow truck approached the Ridge Riders Lodge. The loud click-click of the blinker sounded, as I caught sight of a figure out the driver's side passenger window. Even though it was off in the distance, the hazy figure looked tall and appeared to float above the ground. I gasped and wished I hadn't when my sister snapped her head around in my direction.

"What?"

"Nothing. I realized we're here already."

"That isn't why, Jeremiah," Millie whispered. "It was the skeleton. You were looking out the window."

"Hush, you two," Mom scolded as the tow truck pulled up in front of the plush lodge.

Saved by mom's interference, I breathed a sigh of relief as one by one we climbed out of the big rig.

Dad told the driver where to deliver the car, while Mom and I carried our bags to the covered entry way near the office.

"Cool! I've always wanted to stay here. Hey, Millie!" I wanted to take her mind off our conversation inside the truck. "Check out the pool. I wish we brought swim suits." She didn't care. She didn't even pester me further about what caught my eye.

That girl could squeeze the joy out of any moment by dwelling on everything wrong. But even I had to admit there was plenty wrong tonight. Like our car riding off on the big flat bed tow truck pulling out onto the highway.

As we gathered near the doorway, a light came on inside the office. Through the glass-paned door, we watched a scruffy looking man fiddling with the lock.

He got the door unlocked and greeted us with a smile, which was nice since we most likely got him out of bed. He hadn't even run a comb through his hair.

"I've been expecting you." He smiled and picked up two of our bags, carrying them inside. Dad and Mom followed him.

"What did that mean?" I whispered to Millie. She was crying when I looked at her.

CHAPTER 24

Millie

"Let's get some ice cream," Jeremiah said. He pointed to the bright neon ice cream sign flashing in the darkness.

She shrugged. "I don't want any. I'm too upset about everything. I still want to know who Boyd Colston is and why he's messing up my adoption."

"Oh man, Millie, you don't let a single discouraging thing out of that brain of yours." Jeremiah tugged on her arm. "Come on, Mom and Dad are in there getting a room and I see a big ice cream display over in the corner."

Millie didn't budge. She plopped down on a picnic bench close to the door. Who cares what Jeremiah wants, she thought. He has nothing to be worried about like I do. His adoption is final. No one can take him away. He looked like he was giving up on her as he reached for the handle to the door.

Millie wiped at more tears. She was exhausted and just wanted to sleep. Maybe forever. She dropped her head to rest on the table when she heard a sudden shout from Jeremiah. "Millie!" Her head jolted back up in alarm.

"What?" she grumbled.

"They have mint chocolate chip ice cream!" He had a big silly grin. "Mint chocolate chip, Millie. You've never in your life passed up mint chocolate chip."

She had to admit, that sounded good right now. He was right. She never could turn down her favorite flavor.

"I see a smile." Jeremiah teased. He came closer, like he was planning on dragging her into the store if she didn't get up on her own power.

Later Millie reveled in the sweet creamy taste of the light green ice cream. She crunched on the extra large chocolate bits while enjoying the plushness of the bed and pillows she leaned back on. "I can't believe a lodge in the middle of nowhere has such luxurious rooms."

They all nodded as they each enjoyed their own favorite flavors. "The store is awesome. So many kinds of ice cream."

"Obviously," Mom said, in between bites, "whoever is in charge, is a big fan of ice cream."

"I knew we should have come here a long time ago." Jeremiah scraped the bottom of his container and licked the last bite off the spoon.

"Well, we're here now." Dad looked rested and content as he stretched out his long legs in the reclining chair.

Mom sat straight up and looked at her. "Millie, I just remembered what you said earlier about hearing the realtor say something on the phone."

Dad swallowed the last bite of his rocky road and looked over at her. "What made you so suspicious of him?"

Millie set her ice cream container down and threw herself into repeating what she'd already told Jeremiah.

"Hmm," her Dad said. "I agree that sounds strange, but I just can't imagine he would risk causing an accident."

"Yes," Mom added. "If what you suspected was true, he could be in trouble with the law and lose his real estate license."

"I just know what I heard." Millie resumed eating her ice cream.

"Well, thank you for sharing it with us," Dad said. "We'll keep it in mind, if other unusual things come up with this property purchase."

The room grew quiet as they finished their snacks and lost themselves in contemplating the day's events.

Millie glanced at the clock on the nightstand when Dad's phone squawked out a text notification. Why would someone from his office be texting him after one in the morning? That reminded her, why did the guy downstairs say he had been expecting them?

Before she could pepper Dad with questions, he started laughing and said "Fantastic!"

"What is it, Max?"

"Just that we'll be driving home in style tomorrow. None of you will believe it!" He looked over at Millie with a smile that just wouldn't quit.

How could he be so happy and wide awake this late? She stifled a yawn. It made her happy seeing her dad so happy.

"Spill the beans, Dad." Jeremiah got off the roll-away bed and tossed his ice cream container in the trash.

"That was Naomi." Dad looked over at Mom. "Lucky, she's a night owl!"

"She and Harrison will drive out tomorrow and bring us a car to borrow." Dad had this smile that just wouldn't quit.

He looked at Millie again and then over at Jeremiah. "How would you two like to go for a drive in a cobalt blue Lamborghini SUV?"

"Max! I didn't even know Lamborghini made SUV's!"

Millie was off the bed, jumping up and down, hugging her dad and laughing. "Wow, Dad, just wow!"

"Valued at close to a quarter of a million dollars," Dad added.

"Cobalt blue. I suddenly am in love with that color! And I don't even know what color that is!" Millie fell back on her bed and stared at the ceiling. She loved this life and never wanted it to end.

"Did they pick up that car today, Max?"

"They did. I wasn't sure they would make that happen, but it looks like it all worked out."

"Did who pick up the car?" Millie sat up in the bed and stared at her parents, as if they were speaking a foreign language. "Where is this car coming from? Are we buying it?"

"Whoa there!" Dad said. "This is temporary, while our car is being repaired."

He bent over to take off his shoes while Mom pulled the covers back on their bed. "But it will be fun to drive for a few days. Don't you think, Millie?"

She nodded with half-closed eyes. She had so many more questions, but sleep was overtaking her. The clock looked blurry as she leaned back on the pillow. It looked like 2 a.m.

So many questions. The guy downstairs knowing they were coming, the Boyd dude lurking in her mind, and where did this car really come from?

Dad never answered when she asked. She drifted off to a fitful sleep, wondering if her dad was a part of the nationwide car theft ring she'd heard about in the news.

CHAPTER 25

Jeremiah

The roar worked it's way into my dream. It sounded louder than any motorcycle I'd ever ridden. It revved up once, twice, then again. This wasn't a dream. This was The Car.

I leaped out of bed, ran to the window and saw nearly everyone at the lodge crowding around the magnificent vehicle. The Lamborghini was here.

I heard Dad and Mom stirring across the room. So dead tired when they dropped off to sleep a few hours ago, they didn't even hear the engine's roar.

Slipping over to Dad's side of the bed, I whispered, "Dad, it's here!"

Millie, in the next bed, was sleeping with the blankets over her head and the world blocked out. Mom rolled over and yanked the covers higher over her shoulder. Dad looked at me with groggy eyes. "What time is it?" He grabbed the alarm clock on the nightstand.

"Seven o'clock? We haven't even been asleep five hour." He groaned.

"Yeah, I guess your night owl friend is also an early bird."

"What? Is the car here?"

"It sure is. I'm surprised you didn't hear it. That exhaust sounds like cannon fire." I rubbed my hands together in anticipation.

He jumped up and grabbed clothes, heading to the bathroom. I was too tired to change before dropping off to sleep a few hours ago, so I woke up in the clothes I went to sleep in.

I ran a comb through my hair, threw on my shoes and hat and paced the floor waiting for Dad.

"Sleepy-head finally decided to get up?" A man greeted Dad with a loud voice when we got down to the car. I circled it a dozen times before Dad could get my attention.

"Son, these are my co-workers, Harrison and his wife Naomi.

This is my son Jeremiah. He's just a little excited about our loaner car."

We shook hands. "What are you doing here so early?" Dad asked them. "You working 24-hour shifts these days?"

Naomi had a soft voice that contrasted with her loud husband. "We went into work at 10 last night. The timing of your text message was uncanny. We had just gotten back to the warehouse with the car."

"The client hadn't even been told yet that we had the car," Naomi said. "So when we were texting, we also mentioned you were stranded in the desert and needed a vehicle."

"He was more than happy for us to bring it to you." Harrison patted the car like it was a living creature. "Said you've done more than enough for him."

Dad circled the car for the first time, just as Mom and Millie arrived. Millie's mouth dropped open. "Watch it kid," I said, "you'll be catching flies."

Millie slapped me on the arm and we got into a playful tussle a ways from the car. But not so far that we didn't hear dad mention something about gunshots.

"Did you hear that?" Millie said.

"Yeah." I pointed to the car. "They're all staring at the back window." I edged my way toward them, not wanting to draw attention.

"Had some trouble here?" Dad sounded concerned.

Harrison shrugged. "Just a few shots."

Dad ran his hand over a couple spots on the back window. "Bulletproof?"

"That's what the spec sheet said."

"Glad you got away."

"Some slick driving and plenty of power were our tickets to freedom." Naomi patted her husband on the back.

"Not to mention, we knew the area better than they did. An alley here, a shortcut there, and we lost them no problem." Harrison added to the get-away story.

"That's why we're here so early," Naomi said. "Rather than risk them finding the warehouse, this remote location was better."

I turned to look at Millie. "Did you hear that?" I mouthed the words.

Her eyes were bulging. I'm guessing she heard.

Harrison dropped keys into Dad's hands. An old Cadillac was parked next to the Lamborghini. "Our shift is over, so we'll be going." They hopped into the other car and took off.

Dad put his arm around Mom's shoulders. "I'm starving. Let's take this car for a spin!"

As Mom and Dad headed for the stairway Millie appeared at my side. "Do you think that is a stolen car?" she whispered.

CHAPTER 26

Millie

"Millie! Why would you say something like that?"

"Don't you listen to the news?" she asked him. "Auto theft is a big thing. It's suspicious this expensive car with bullet holes just shows up." She glared at him. "Figure it out. The pieces add up."

Jeremiah shook his head. "No, the pieces don't add up. Especially one big piece you're leaving out."

"And what is that, Mr. Know-it-All?"

"Our dad is not a car thief."

But how do we really know? Millie thought. She didn't say more though. Jeremiah already thought she was a worrywart, and he didn't even know half the things going on inside her head. Sometimes she couldn't believe these parents were as good as they seemed. She had lived with families where stolen cars would have been no big deal. In fact her own family, not that she remembered much about them, but she'd heard stories from social workers and foster families. They supported themselves by stealing anything they could find. That and selling drugs.

"Well, I didn't say he stole the car, but he could be involved with people who did."

"Let's go eat breakfast. We're tired, yesterday was rough. Later we'll get some answers from Dad that will put your mind at ease." He tugged on her arm and headed toward the stairs.

"You better not tell him what I said."

"I'm not that stupid. Now come on!"

The Lamborghini was beyond luxurious and Millie couldn't help but sink into the plush back seat, while she looked around in awe at the rest of the interior. The sound system was out of this world and her favorite Christian music permeated the air so thoroughly she couldn't tell where the speakers were. "Funny how Christian music would come on in a stolen car," she whispered to Jeremiah. Then she thought, maybe God does stuff like that to make criminals feel guilty.

"You're a goofball." Jeremiah said.

Millie looked over at him, but he was looking out the side window.

"Dad! Check out the license plate on that truck."

They all looked where he pointed and Millie read, "Minnesota... Hey!"

Dad and Jeremiah burst out laughing.

"I don't believe it." Dad smacked his forehead. "It's our good buddy."

"Well, I guess if his truck is still here when we get back, we'll pay him a visit." Dad pulled the luxury car onto the two-lane highway.

"I'm looking forward to that." Mom smiled at Jeremiah. "You've told such wonderful tales, I just have to meet this man."

"I want to hear what he has to say about the skeleton and the gold," Millie said. "Let's hurry and get back!"

The car filled with laughter as they covered the 40 miles between the lodge and the restaurant.

At the restaurant Millie wanted answers but found it difficult to ask her dad anything. And she sure didn't want to let on to her mom she had seen Boyd's name on the laptop. She started with something safe.

"Mom." She cut her French toast and slathered it with syrup while she talked. "Why did that guy say he was expecting us last night when we got there?"

"Yeah," Jeremiah joined in. "That was weird, like someone was telling him about us."

Mom smiled. "Someone was," she said and took a sip of her orange juice.

"See, Jeremiah." Millie thumped his arm with the back of her hand. "I told you weird things were going on."

Jeremiah looked like he finally believed her.

"Oh Millie, honey, there's been too much talk of desert legends and far too little sleep. You're seeing mysteries everywhere."

"What do you mean? You said someone was talking to the man about us."

"I'm sorry, honey I shouldn't have teased you. What I meant was, we talked with the man."

Millie still looked confused. "Earlier in the day," Mom said. "After I got the call from the realtor, I made the reservations."

Even Jeremiah looked a little sheepish for believing something strange was happening. Millie was relieved, but she still had so many other questions.

They resumed eating quietly until Millie broke the silence. "But what about the car?"

Dad looked up over the edge of the iced tea he was drinking. "What do you want to know about the car?" he said as he set his glass down.

"Why does it have bullet holes and where did it come from?"

CHAPTER 27

Jeremiah

I just about spit my apple juice out when I heard the questions that rushed out of my sister's mouth.

Dad smiled at her. "Well, you don't want to know much, do you?"

Oh, if you only knew, Dad, I was thinking, but I didn't want to get Millie started on anything else.

"Well?" Millie said.

"You might say it's a company car we're borrowing."

If he was hoping to put Millie off with a vague answer like that, well, as the saying goes, he had another think coming.

"What do you mean. 'you might say?'"

Dad took a deep breath and looked at Mom. "It's up to you," she said.

"Actually Millie, it would be easier to explain the skeleton in the desert to you than to get into the details about the company car."

"Well, I want to know that story too. But I'm curious about the car. And I want to know about the company too."

My sister looked over at me. "Do you even know what Dad does when he goes to work?"

Hmm. "Now that you mention it, I guess I don't." I realized right then and there, I am no way as curious about every detail in life as Millie is. "I know he works for RPM something or other." Maybe I would score some points with my vast knowledge and big smile.

"Works for or owns the company?" she asked.

I looked across the table at Dad and Mom who seemed to enjoy this, then back at my sister. "Well, I guess I never thought of it."

"That's the problem with you, Jeremiah. You never wonder about anything."

"Oh. I didn't know that was a problem. And may I point out one of your problems?" Without waiting for her answer, I said "You not only wonder about every little detail in the world, you also worry about it. Constantly!" I stared at her for emphasis.

"He's right, you know." Mom reached across the table and patted her hand.

"It's good to want to know what's going on," Dad said. "But we need to help you put a stop to the worry."

Millie hung her head. If I had to guess, I would say she was torn between admitting they were right and wanting to get back to the question that started this whole conversation.

She looked up at Dad. "Okay. If I promise to stop worrying so much, will you tell me about the car we 'might say' is a company car?"

As he was about to respond, his phone vibrated on the table. He glanced at the caller ID then back at us. "Excuse me." He stood and stepped away from the table. "I need to take this. It's the sheriff's office."

Millie and I stared at each other as Dad walked out of the restaurant.

CHAPTER 28

Millie

Millie could feel her insides shaking. She fidgeted and fretted so much on the drive back to the lodge she couldn't enjoy the surround sound and plush upholstery.

"I won't know what to say, Dad. I'm too scared."

"You sound like Moses in the Bible," Jeremiah said.

"Be quiet." She glared at him. "You're not the one who has to talk to the deputy."

"This is one time where your attention to every little detail is good. And bad."

"Why do you say that?" She looked at her brother.

"Because you know what that guy looks like, so that's good. And it's bad for you because you're the one the deputy wants to talk to."

She frowned.

"Take me for instance, I didn't notice anything during the wreck, so they don't need me."

"Well, I wish I was you," Millie held her stomach and rocked forward and back. It had been a long time since she had done that. She had a vague memory of rocking and rocking when she was a little girl scared and... no, she wouldn't go there. Mom interrupted her thoughts.

"Millie, you'll be fine, and Jeremiah is right, you noticing all the details is very helpful. They might catch the guy who ran into us."

The deputy was standing next to his patrol car talking on the radio when they pulled into the nearest parking space.

"Hi, I'm Deputy Black. Mr. Anderson?"

"Yes, good morning." Dad extended his hand. "Thank you for coming out."

Millie could see people in the office looking out, which made her more nervous. She looked around and spotted the truck from

Minnesota and wished they were discussing tales of skeletons and gold instead of answering questions.

"My daughter's a little nervous." Dad put his arm around her.

"Millie, the only one who should be nervous is the creep who wrecked your car and endangered your family." The deputy smiled at her, then pulled his phone out and scrolled to a picture of a dented up car.

"That's it!" Millie blurted out, startling even herself. "I know that car, it's the one that ran into us last night."

"Where did you find it?" Mom asked.

"About 15 miles west of here, abandoned on the side of the highway." He put his phone away and pulled out a small notepad and pen. "It appears he ran out of gas, but how he got out of the area, we don't know."

"Can't you get his name from the car registration?" Jeremiah asked.

"The car was stolen."

Millie's eyes grew wide, and she rolled them to the side to see Jeremiah without turning her head. She hoped this proved to him she knew what she was talking about when she said there was a rash of car thefts.

She just hoped her dad's company wasn't involved. It seemed risky to have the deputy so close to the Lamborghini with the bullet holes. Thankfully, he wasn't paying attention to it.

After she described the man, and her parents answered questions, he shook hands with them. "We'll have the report ready in a few days." He handed her dad a business card. "Just check with my office and you can get a copy for your insurance company."

None of them noticed Minnesota Mike standing nearby. When the deputy turned to approach his car, M&M cleared his throat and said, "Well, howdy folks, doncha know, I was hoping we would run into each other again, real soon like!"

Wow, his voice was just as loud as Jeremiah said it was. Millie choked back laughter.

Before the deputy could get into his car, M&M turned his attention from Dad and said "Excuse me there, Deputy. I was hoping to ask you a question."

"Sure, what can I do for you?"

"Well, er, well." He seemed like he didn't know how to get started. "It's kind of a silly question, and I'm not from around here. But can you tell me if there's any truth to the stories I been hearing about a skeleton wandering around at night with a lantern in his belly?"

Jeremiah burst out laughing, attracting everyone's attention. Especially Dad, who did not look happy about his reaction.

The deputy chuckled and said, "You know, ordinarily, I would say that is a silly question, but..." He stopped talking and flipped through the pages on his spiral notepad.

Time seemed to stand still as they all stood speechless at the deputy's reaction.

He found what he was looking for. "Sure enough," he said, reading his notes. "Last week, we got a call from one of the off roaders camping in the area. He claimed while he was out on a night run in his buggy he saw something that looked like a tall skeleton carrying a lantern."

The deputy looked up from his notes. "We chalked it up to a little too much to drink at the local tavern." He looked right at Minnesota Mike. "So, have you seen this skeleton yourself?"

M&M bounced back and forth from one foot to the other and seemed to be searching for an answer. "Well, now, I ain't saying I saw it myself for sure."

The deputy closed his notepad, slipping it back into his top pocket. "Okay, big fellow, well, you keep an eye out and if you ever see it, just let me know."

He got into his patrol car and the engine roared to life. Before driving off, he rolled the window down and said to M&M, "You be careful about driving after you've been to the tavern, you hear?"

Chapter 29

Jeremiah

Minnesota Mike let out a loud belly laugh as the deputy drove off. When he could catch his breath, he turned to Dad. "He must think I'm a drinker to believe a story like that."

Dad smiled. "Well, it is far-fetched to think an old desert legend has come to life in modern times."

"Oh, I don't doubt what you're saying." Minnesota looked in my direction. "But I betcha Jeremiah wouldn't think so if he coulda seen what I saw late last night after I checked in here." He motioned over his shoulder with his thumb.

"What did you see?" Millie butted into the conversation before I could respond.

"Just like I told the deputy..."

"Wait a minute," Millie interrupted. "You told the deputy you didn't see anything." She pointed her finger right at him and squinted her eyes. "Were you lying?"

That girl will be an investigator or maybe even a judge someday. She doesn't stop till she gets to the truth.

"Millie, Jeremiah," Dad inserted himself into the conversation. "We're meeting someone in town this afternoon, so we need to get packed." He looked in M&M's direction. "It was nice seeing you again."

Dad motioned for both of us to follow him. Mom smiled in Minnesota's direction. "Maybe we can visit another time." She turned and headed for the stairway.

"Oh, sure, yeah, okay," Minnesota waved. "Don't let me hold you up. By the way, that's a right nice ride you got there. Sure is a step up from the truck you was in yesterday."

"Thank you," Dad said, "it's borrowed from a friend."

"Oh, okay." M&M smiled. "Well, I know some tricks to repair auto glass if you want me to help you with those bullet holes in the back."

I could see Dad gritting his teeth. This guy had such a way of getting under Dad's skin, but he played it cool. "I'll mention that to my friend," he said and walked away.

"Well, now hold on there, just one more second." M&M hurried after us while digging around in his pocket. He pulled out a crumpled looking business card. "Lookie here. Keep this with you in case your friend wants help. It's got my number scribbled on the back."

He gave me the card since I was closest to him. I read "Amos Lee, Realtor" .

"Oh, that ain't me." Minnesota saw me reading the card. "I got that from that realtor guy down the road. I put my number on the back for you folks, then forgot to give it to you yesterday."

"Okay, thank you." Dad motioned to me. "Come on, Jeremiah."

I felt bad shutting Minnesota down like that. He was a nice guy, even if he had some strange ideas.

"Say, I heard you put your offer in on that property," he yelled as we started up the stairs.

No secrets in this town.

Dad kept going.

"You might want to hear to what I have to say, before you sign any agreement to buy."

I wanted to stay and hear the story but knew I better not, so I waved and hurried to catch up with the rest of the family. It surprised me Millie was so content to just walk away from this gold mine of information.

What was up with her?

It didn't take long to find out.

CHAPTER 30

Millie

Millie was crying so hard she couldn't talk. Her dad and mom were both trying to comfort her when Jeremiah walked in.

"Whoa! What is going on?"

She looked at her brother, but couldn't stop crying.

Mom brought over a wet washcloth and wiped her face.

"Millie, honey, please. Try to be calm and tell us what is wrong."

"Take deep breaths, Millie." Her dad rubbed her back. That always helped when she was like this.

She was so grateful for these parents. She didn't know what she would have done if they hadn't come into her life. That caused the tears to flow harder, as she thought about the problems with her adoption.

"Deep breaths, Millie," Dad said. "You were doing good for a minute."

Mom took the cloth. "Let me run this under cold water again."

She wiped Millie's face when she came back. "Honey, what's wrong? Did something happen downstairs to upset you?"

The tears subsided as she continued to inhale and breathe out like her dad said. "Well," she started.

"It was probably Minnesota Mike carrying on," Jeremiah said. "He's enough to make any of us cry."

"It was when he talked about the bullet holes." Her tears started again. Why is it so hard to talk when you're crying? She looked over at Jeremiah. "You tell him," she squeaked.

Her parents looked surprised. "Me? Why me? I'm not even the one wondering about the car."

"Jeremiah?" Dad looked his way. "Do you know what's bothering her?"

75

"Yes." He took a deep breath. "She thinks the Lamborghini is stolen."

"Stolen!" Mom jumped to her feet. "Why on earth would you think it's stolen, Millie?"

Dad put his arm around her shoulders and hugged her to his side. She still couldn't talk and stared in Jeremiah's direction.

"Millie doesn't know what your job is, and she thinks it's strange that an expensive car shows up with bullet holes in it. She's been hearing in the news about car theft rings." Jeremiah let out a sigh of relief when he finished.

"Thank you," she whispered.

"Max, tell them about your job." Mom put her hand on their dad's shoulder.

"You know, it's funny." Dad shook his head a little. "You think you're protecting your kids by keeping some things from them, but instead you're making them more worried."

Yeah, like what's going on with my adoption? Millie wondered, but decided that could wait for another time.

"When people buy expensive cars, they borrow money from a lender to pay for it," Dad said.

"What does that have to do with bullet holes in the car?" Millie interrupted.

Dad smiled. "I'm getting to that."

He took a drink from the cold water bottle Mom handed him.

"Can I have one too, Mom?" Millie said.

"The borrower makes payments every month. But if they don't, the lender will repossess their vehicle."

"What does that mean?"

"It means it's getting taken away from them," Jeremiah said.

"Is that right, Dad?"

"Yes it is. When that happens, some borrowers are cooperative, but others aren't. They'll hide the car to keep the lender from taking it back."

"And, somehow, this is getting us to the bullet holes?" Millie asked in between gulps of water.

"Yes. And that's why I don't talk about my work at home. It can be dangerous. The items we specialize in are very expensive. Yachts, airplanes, luxury vehicles. Sometimes people go to great lengths to stop us from taking the vehicles."

Millie opened her mouth to speak, but Dad shushed her with his hand held up. "Let me finish."

"Someone shot at my coworkers last night when they were recovering the Lamborghini for our client."

Jeremiah and Millie gasped. "Dad! That could have been you," Millie said.

"Not anymore. I don't work in the field any longer. I haven't for quite some time."

"What if that guy who hit our car knew who you were? What if he was following you to hurt you?"

She saw her Dad glance over at her mom.

"Millie," Dad said. "You're jumping to conclusions. Let's stick with what we know."

Millie looked at her mom, who was still staring at her dad. It looked like she thought there was something to the idea about the man hunting for Dad.

"How did your coworkers keep from getting hurt when the people shot at them?" Jeremiah asked.

"It's bulletproof glass. The bullets never pierced the window. We knew about that safety feature, because it was in the paperwork we got from our client."

Millie jumped up and threw her arms around her dad, hugging him. "Oh Dad! I'm so glad you're not a car thief!"

"Oh brother, Millie!" Jeremiah shook his head. "Crying because you're upset. Crying because you're happy."

"But what about Mom? Did she know about all this?" She turned to her mom. "Did you, Mom?"

"Yes, honey. I also work for your Dad's company."

"What do you do?"

"She does the research on people we're hunting for. To find out as much as we can about them."

Jeremiah stared over at Millie and then turned to their Mom. "You mean like background checks on people?"

"That is some of the research I do."

Without looking at him, Millie could feel Jeremiah's eyes boring a hole into her. She knew just what he was thinking.

CHAPTER 31

Jeremiah

"Hey, Dad, how soon are we leaving? Is it okay for us to look around the lodge first?"

I couldn't wait to talk to Millie away from our parents. I wanted to make sure she would stop worrying about that Boyd guy now.

"Sure, son. In fact, I'm going to cancel that appointment this afternoon. I think we'll stay another day."

"Oh, cool!" Millie jumped up. "Let's go."

As we got to the door, Dad said, "If you see good old M&M, tell him we'd like to have lunch with him later in the cafe here."

"Wow. Really, Dad?" I couldn't believe my ears.

"Yes, I feel kind of bad for the way I've been giving him the brush off." He looked over at Mom. "Besides your mom told me I had to."

That sounded like something Mom would make him do.

"When you get back up here," Mom added, "we'll drive over to the realtor's office to see if he has any word on our offer."

"Wow, double wow! What a great day this is turning out to be."

"We'll be back soon," Millie said, as we headed out the door.

We almost tripped over each other rushing down the stairs. There was so much I wanted to see here, but I was also looking forward to news from the realtor.

"How about we just check out the pool, then find M&M, and get right back after that?"

"That's the same thing I was thinking," Millie agreed. "There's plenty of time to explore later, and if we get that property, we'll have the rest of our lives to explore."

At the pool, two men stormed through the wooden gate, almost running into us. They were arguing. They were talking too quietly to make out the words, but you could tell it was an argument by the tone of their voices and hand gestures. They didn't even notice us.

"What do you think that was about?" Millie whispered.

"I don't know, but they sure were mad." I followed her into the pool area.

"Check out those rooms, Millie." I pointed across the patio area. "They have sliding glass doors leading right out to the pool."

"That would be cool to stay in. We should ask Dad if we can do that the next time we come here."

The sound of motorcycles racing around in the desert nearby made me wish we had brought ours. An old dune buggy with two people in it chugged along the dirt road by the pool heading toward the open desert. Maybe we'd get a buggy when we moved into our new desert home. That way the whole family could go out together.

I was just about to tell Millie my idea when she motioned me to follow her around the large patio area. As we got to the other side of the pool, the angry voices we'd heard earlier sounded close. This time they weren't so quiet.

"I think they're in one of those rooms," Millie whispered.

"Yeah, I think you're right."

She sat on a cushioned recliner at the pool's edge. One that was closest to the room with the loud voices. Millie stretched out like a sunbather who would be here for a while.

"What are you doing? I thought we were in a hurry to find Mike and get back to Dad and Mom?"

"Shh." She held her finger to her lips. Then in a louder voice, "Come on, Jeremiah, let's enjoy the sun." She patted the reclining lounge next to her.

I was just about to tell her no when we heard a loud noise, like someone knocking over a table. Then yelling. "I told you that idiot would talk about the gold!"

I plopped down so fast on the lounge next to her, I almost tipped over. She laughed.

"Shush! We don't want them to hear us."

There was more yelling but not loud enough to make out the words.

Something crashed against one of the glass doors. It surprised me the window didn't shatter. "And that's just what I'll do to that old geezer if I hear one more time he's blabbing about that property."

Silence. We strained our ears to listen, but they had either left the room or quit talking.

"Millie, did you hear that?"

"Yes!" Her whisper was louder than mine. "You think they're talking about M&M?"

"I bet they are and I bet they're talking about our property."

"Who are they?" she said "And I wonder where M&M is now."

"He sure didn't seem to be in the room the way they were talking about him."

"No, it wasn't like they were talking to him, just about him," she said.

"It almost seems like there is something to that gold story he's been talking about, for as mad as those guys were."

"Do you think Mike is in danger?" Millie looked scared. I hoped she wouldn't cry again.

"I don't know, but I think we should tell Mom and Dad what we heard."

"No, Jeremiah. Let's wait till we find out more. We've had enough trouble today."

"Oh yeah." I remembered what I came outside to talk to her about. "Speaking of trouble, you can quit worrying about that Boyd guy now. Did you hear what Dad said about Mom's background checks for his company?"

Millie looked sheepish, and so she should. Once again she was making a mountain out of a molehill. To use my Dad's words.

"Yes, you're right. I worry too much."

"Yeah, so now you can cross Boyd off your worry list."

"Okay. I'll cross Boyd off and add Minnesota Mike's name. He might be in some kind of trouble."

I had the same bad feeling.

CHAPTER 32

Millie

"Let's go ask in the office what room M&M is in," Millie said as they left the pool area.

"No! It's probably the room those men were in."

"Yeah, I guess you could be right. Let's at least wander around the store. We might overhear something while we're in there."

"It pays to hang out with the master eavesdropper when we need information." Jeremiah smiled at his sister.

She pushed the door open and the desk clerk greeted them. They hadn't seen her before.

"Hi there, what can I do for you?" She was friendly, young and tan. Like she spent every waking moment out by the swimming pool when she wasn't working. You could do that out here in the desert. The sun was shining 360 days a year, Millie thought.

"We thought we'd check out all your cool items," Jeremiah said while Millie stared at her. "We're in room 201."

"Oh, you're the Lamborghini. Awesome car!" She gave two thumbs up.

"Yeah, no kidding," Jeremiah said. "It's a loaner since ours got wrecked last night."

"Wow, you guys made out on that deal!"

"How old are you?" Millie could tell that annoyed Jeremiah. Someday maybe she'd stop being so blunt, but right now it was the only way she knew to get information.

"Fifteen in six more months." The girl smiled. She didn't seem to mind being questioned.

"How come you're not in school?"

"Millie, do you have to interrogate her?"

"I don't think two questions is an interrogation."

The counter girl laughed at the brother and sister bickering. "It's okay, I know how it is, I've got a little brother, and someone is always annoyed with someone else in our house."

Then she answered Millie's question. "Homeschool."

"Awesome!" both Jeremiah and Millie responded.

"Same here," Millie said.

"By the way, my name is Paisley." She held her hand across the counter and shook their hands.

"So what are you guys doing out here? You don't have a truck or trailer, so I doubt you're doing any riding."

"Not this trip," Jeremiah said. "Hopefully we'll be back in a week or two with the bikes."

"Yeah, we're just here with our parents to..."

Jeremiah cut her off. "We just went for a desert drive, got in a wreck and ended up staying all night."

Millie gave him a puzzled look, but decided he must have a good reason for stopping her.

"That's cool you got the loaner car delivered to you." Paisley stared out the window at the Lamborghini. "Must have some great connections."

"I guess." Jeremiah stared out the window.

"Say," Millie jumped in to redirect the conversation. "Have you seen the guy around that goes by the name of Minnesota Mike?"

"That old guy?" Paisley chuckled. "Happiest guy I've ever seen, except..."

"Except what?" Millie interrupted.

"I haven't seen him today. But his truck is parked in the same spot."

"We saw him not too long ago," Jeremiah said.

"I haven't seen him since I came on duty an hour ago." Paisley tapped on the keyboard, staring at the screen as she scrolled through several pages. "He's scheduled to check out today, but he's already missed the check-out time."

Jeremiah and Millie looked at each other as Paisley punched numbers into her phone. "Excuse me. I need to check with my dad."

She waited a minute or two, then it sounded like she was leaving a message. "Can you check on Room 110? He should have checked out an hour ago, but I haven't seen him."

"Is he a friend of yours?" Paisley continued looking at the computer.

"Well, not really. More like an acquaintance. My dad and brother met him yesterday."

"Same here." Paisley still didn't look up from the computer screen while she talked. "He checked in late yesterday afternoon while I was on duty. I was doing my schoolwork since it was slow and he kept popping in and out of the store all afternoon and evening. Asked me a thousand questions about school and then told me a thousand stories about wandering around the country."

"He's a character, all right," Jeremiah agreed. "But as you said, a friendly one."

"You got that right." Paisley picked up the phone again as if hoping it would ring.

"My dad and I went for a ride with him yesterday. He must have checked into his room after we left for home."

Paisley looked up when he said that. "Wait a minute, you left for home yesterday but then you checked in here late last night." She glanced back at the computer, scrolling through the info, then looked back at them. "Actually, early this morning. You must have done a lot of driving yesterday."

Jeremiah and Millie laughed. "Yeah, long story."

Before Paisley could ask any more questions, the phone rang. "Saved by the bell," Millie whispered as the girl took the call. It sounded like her dad by the one-sided conversation.

"She asks as many questions as you do," Jeremiah whispered.

"Yeah, how annoying."

"What, Dad?" her voice raised, "Are you sure? Did you call 9-1-1?"

She punched the off button on her phone and stared at Jeremiah and Millie. "My dad said he's on his floor, unconscious." Her voice was quivering.

They heard the siren before they saw the fire truck.

As the three of them rushed outside, Millie saw the man who had checked them in last night, signaling the driver where to go.

"Millie! Jeremiah!" Their parents were outside. "We were afraid something happened to you." Her mom put an arm around Millie's shoulders. "What is it, honey?"

"It's Minnesota Mike, Mom. Something terrible happened."

CHAPTER 33

Jeremiah

Dad put an arm around both of us. "Let's step over here and pray for Mike."

We moved away from the small crowd that was growing. An ambulance pulled in and parked next to the fire truck.

"Lord, we don't know what is going on with our new friend Mike, but You do. Please touch Him with your healing hand and breathe health and life into his body. Please give the paramedics wisdom to know what to do. Show us how we can be a blessing to Mike and all those involved."

When I looked up, I saw them wheeling an awake and talking Minnesota Mike out of his hotel room. Millie and I rushed over. "Hey there." M&M reached out a feeble hand for mine. He was talking all right, but not with the exuberance of yesterday.

"What kind of trouble are you causing everyone?" I walked along as they rolled him over to the ambulance. "You get beat up by some friends?" I was only half kidding and looked around to see if the two men were in the crowd that had formed.

Minnesota looked up at me with what I would call a startled look. I could tell by his reaction there was something to that argument we heard earlier.

He shook his head and smiled. "Not today. Too much pop and not enough water, I guess."

"Really?" Millie said.

"Dehydration," he said. Mike's strength was gone. But he held onto my hand.

"Are you folks family?" The attendant looked at my dad who stood next to us.

"Friends." It was amazing how much had changed since we first saw Mike on the highway yesterday morning. "Is he going to be okay?"

"Well, I'm only supposed to be talking to family…"

"Oh go on, you young whippersnapper." M&M summoned the strength to scold the attendant who was young enough to be his grandson. "Tell my good friends here the whole story. They're the only ones I got to trust and help me right now."

Mike winked at me as he talked, his voice trailing off to a whisper.

"He is severely dehydrated. His blood pressure had dropped too. Apparently he stood up too fast and passed out, then hit his head on a table when he fell. We're not sure how long he was out when we got the call."

"We saw him not more than an hour ago," Mom said.

"It's a good thing we got to him so soon."

They loaded him into the ambulance and Mike called out, "You make sure my friends know where you're taking me, you hear? I need them there." He looked me right in the eye. "I got somethin' important I need to discuss with you, Jeremiah."

I noticed a key hanging on a chain around his neck. Mike saw me and moved his hand up to his chest. He took hold of the key. "Yep, something mighty important I need to discuss with you."

He closed his eyes and drifted off as they shut the ambulance doors.

I turned to Millie, but the sight of the men we had seen arguing, standing off in the distance, made me forget what I was going to say.

CHAPTER 34

Millie

"Drive faster, Dad!" Millie urged as the ambulance pulled away from them on the highway. "We may not find the hospital if we're not right behind them!"

"In this car?" her Dad said. "Doubt that." He pointed to the GPS tracking map on the dash. "Mom has already put in the hospital's name."

"Besides, getting stopped for speeding would take us even longer," Jeremiah said.

"This looks like the way to the restaurant." Millie watched the hard-packed desert racing past their side windows. An occasional group of motorcycles or quads ripping along the washes and jumping the hills in the distance made her wish they were on their dirt bikes having fun. Not dealing with so many problems.

"Yes, it is," Dad said. "The hospital is about 10 miles past the town where we ate."

"That seems like so long ago." Millie stared out the window, rubbing her chin and worrying. It was her specialty.

Dad checked in at the front desk. The waiting room was noisy and crowded with most of the chairs full. Millie thought sure she could hear M&M talking each time the door opened to admit someone to the emergency room. He must be feeling stronger already.

"They said it will be a few minutes." Dad looked at Mom. "This is kind of unusual, but Mike only wants Millie and Jeremiah to visit."

"Max!" Mom sounded like she didn't agree.

"The doctor said that could help calm him." Dad looked over at Millie and Jeremiah, then back to Mom. "They're concerned he will escalate to an anxiety attack on top of the dehydration. They noticed his heart rate going up when the doctor said adults only."

Jeremiah looked at Millie and leaned close. "The plot thickens."

She had to hold back laughter.

"Let's take a seat while we wait." Mom motioned to a row of chairs.

Millie paced the floor, thinking about the information Mike had for them. Maybe he'd tell them where the gold was. Or if the skeleton was real. Or who those men were.

As she paced, she noticed an older woman in a wheelchair watching her. Every time she walked one way, her gray head turned and followed her. When she walked back, the woman's head turned that way. Millie stopped in front of her.

"This is Miss Nita."

The voice startled Millie. She saw a woman sitting next to the wheelchair. "Is she sick?"

"She has dementia." The woman looked sad. "It's where your mind stops working." She touched Miss Nita's cheek. "She's my mother. I'm Ivy."

Millie knelt down and looked into Miss Nita's eyes. "Hi, there!" she said.

"Oh my goodness!" Ivy said when Miss Nita smiled. "I haven't seen her smile in weeks!"

"She's sweet." Millie took hold of Miss Nita's hand. It was clenched shut. She held Miss Nita's fist. "What's wrong with her hand?"

"She holds it like that." Ivy placed her hand on top of Millie's. "Sometimes I pry her hand open to trim her fingernails."

"Does she let you?"

Ivy laughed. "You wouldn't believe how strong she is. She fights me, but I win."

"Visitors for Mike Bailey." A nurse stood by the emergency room door.

"I'll see you later, Miss Nita." Millie said.

Before Millie and Jeremiah crossed the waiting room, the men from the hotel stepped over to the nurse. "That would be us."

The nurse looked at the chart. "I don't think so." She looked back at them. "You're not Millie and Jeremiah."

"Hey, Mike is our brother!" one of them barked out. "Family before strangers."

"Take that up with the front desk."

"Do you think they are brothers?" Millie whispered to Jeremiah as they followed the nurse past a lot of beds with curtains around them.

"Beats me," Jeremiah said, "but we're about to find out!"

CHAPTER 35

Jeremiah

"Well, lookie here, if it ain't my best buddies on the planet." Minnesota Mike's voice was weak. Tubes taped to his hand were connected to machines near his bed.

"Well, I'll be." The nurse was looking at a monitor by the bed. "You really are good for him, his heartbeat slowed."

I took Mike's hand and pointed in Millie's direction. "Not sure you met my mouthy sister." I felt a sharp jab in my ribs as I was about to introduce the source of that jab.

"Hey! Don't call me mouthy."

"Well, little lady. Iff'n the shoe fits, as they say." He chuckled and I joined in.

"Anyway, this is Millie."

"Just a few minutes now." The nurse pulled the curtain shut and left.

"Come in here, close-like." M&M motioned for them to lean down. "I got to get this key to you real fast before our time runs out."

I looked at the key still hanging around his chest. He fumbled with it and Millie reached over to help with the clasp.

"You take this and hang onto it for me. I can't afford to lose it and these hospital people keep trying to take it off me. Says it's in their way."

Millie slipped it into the pocket of her jeans. "What's the key for?"

"I can't go into that now, but I can tell you there's a couple guys who want it bad."

Millie's eyes grew wide as she looked away from M&M and over at me.

"I think I know what guys you're talking about," I said. "We heard them arguing at the lodge."

"Oh, you heard that, did ya?"

"Is that why you're in here?" Millie butted in.

M&M looked at me. "She don't mince words none, now does she?"

"Well, is it?" Millie ignored the comment.

"Actually, Mike, I'm kind of wondering that myself."

"Well if ya can keep a secret, I'll tell you."

We both nodded.

"They took me by surprise and got into my room when I was heading back from talking with you and that deputy."

"What did they want?" I prodded.

"I don't want to go into all that, but I knowed for sure they want this key. They was searching my room."

"What were you talking about when you told my dad I'd be interested in what you saw last night?"

"Oh, that," M&M waved his hand in the air. "That's not as important as what I got to talk to you about now."

The nurse popped her head in through the curtains, "Five minutes and then we're taking him to x-ray."

"Thank you." Millie answered for all of us.

"Anyways, they ended up shoving me a little too hard and when I fell, I guess I hit my head on a table and got knocked out. They must'a high-tailed it outta there. But they didn't get my key."

"What should we do with it?" Millie asked the question we both were wondering.

"Well, you jist hang onto it for me. You got my number in case I don't get out before you all leave the lodge. I know we'll see each other again soon, I just feel it in my bones. But whatever you do, ya gotta protect that key."

"Can't you give us a hint what it's for?" I said.

"Nah, it's just too dang long of a story."

He rested his head back against the pillow and closed his eyes. His breathing was steady and deep.

We heard the curtains rustling. A different attendant stepped in and checked the wires and tubes.

M&M opened his eyes at the sound and winked at both of us. "There's danger out there. Don't lose that key," he whispered.

We stepped aside and watched as the attendant wheeled him away in his bed.

Minutes later we pushed open the door to the waiting room and came face-to-face with the angry men.

"Did he give you that key?" The loud demanding voice attracted the attention of everyone in the waiting room.

CHAPTER 36

Millie

Millie looked past the two men, relieved to see Miss Nita and Ivy still waiting their turn. She knew what to do.

Before she or Jeremiah could respond, her Dad intervened. "Don't talk to my kids that way!" Wow, she had never heard him sound so angry.

Millie edged away as the armed security guard joined her dad.

She could hear the rumble of their voices, as she hurried across the waiting room and knelt in front of Miss Nita.

"Are you okay, dear?" Ivy said to her.

Millie nodded and stared up into Miss Nita's eyes. "Hi there!"

Miss Nita's face lit up, and she shocked Millie when she spoke in a husky, monotone, "Hi."

"Wow!" Millie looked over at Miss Nita's daughter. "Did you hear that?"

"You are a gift from heaven." She hugged Millie. "She hasn't spoken in weeks." Ivy wiped tears away.

Millie didn't see her approach, but now Mom joined in the hug. As the two women talked, Millie eased her way out of the embrace. She rubbed Miss Nita's clenched fist.

The ladies, and the men still arguing across the room, were so engrossed in their conversations no one noticed Millie slip a key into the elderly fingers she pried open. When she let go, they snapped back into the tight fist, hiding the treasure Mike had entrusted to them.

The voices were dying down across the room and Millie stood up to see what would happen. As she turned, she saw Jeremiah looking her way. He moved next to her. "Well played, sister," he whispered.

She smiled. "Oh, you saw that?"

He nodded, just as the two of them became the center of attention.

"Let's all step outside to talk." Her Dad motioned, as the two men and the security guard watched them. The men headed for the automatic doors at the waiting room entrance.

Millie turned to offer a quick goodbye to Miss Nita. "I have to go talk to my dad, but I'll be right back." She hurried to catch up to her family.

"Your kids have something that belongs to us and we want it right now." The taller man glared at them.

Dad turned to them, "Millie, Jeremiah, these men believe that Mike gave you something of theirs."

Millie looked at her brother, then back to her dad. She shrugged her shoulders. "He didn't give us anything."

"That's not true." The shorter one insisted.

"I don't know how you would know what went on in there," Dad said.

"It's a key, it would be easy for them to hide it."

"Millie," Dad sounded exasperated. "Do you have a key from Mike?"

"Search her! She won't tell. He probably told her what it was for."

"What is it for?" Now Dad looked interested.

"Never mind! Just check her pockets."

"Millie, they have no right to ask, but to keep peace, can you empty your pockets?"

"I'll pull my pockets out and show you they're empty."

She reached in and yanked out both pockets. The only thing they produced were bits of lint.

Before the men could ask, Jeremiah did the same. His pockets were filled with gum and candy wrappers, bullet casings and a couple rubber bands.

"What are you doing with all that junk?" Millie helped him pick up all the trash.

He shrugged. "It's a handy little wastebasket."

The men stormed off. Millie could hear them muttering. "I'm sure he gave those kids that key!"

Dad looked at Mom. "What was that all about?"

Mom chuckled. "I don't know, but it goes right along with how our week is going."

Dad put his arm around her shoulder and looked toward the kids, "How about we head back and check in with the realtor?"

"Wait a sec, Dad." Millie turned toward the door. "I promised Miss Nita I'd tell her goodbye."

"I'll bring the car around." Dad headed to the parking lot.

"Oh, no!" Millie stood near the empty chair where she last saw Ivy. There was no sign of her or Miss Nita in her wheelchair.

"What do I do now?" She moaned and plopped down into the empty chair.

CHAPTER 37

Jeremiah

"Jeremiah, go see what's keeping your sister." Mom watched Dad pull the car to the nearby curb.

I hurried through the automatic doors and at first didn't even see Millie. Then I took a second look around the waiting room.

"Millie! What are you doing just sitting there?"

She lifted her head from her hands and looked up at me. "I've lost the key, Jeremiah." She whimpered and dropped her gaze back to the floor.

This girl! How was I ever going to survive till she got through this emotional time of her life? Or maybe girls never get through it. Who knew?

"Did you drop it?"

"No." She whimpered more. "The ladies weren't here." She looked at me. "I asked at the front desk if I could talk to Ivy and they said no."

"No? That's it, they just said 'no' with no reason?"

"I don't remember, I was too upset."

This girl needed to learn a little more about perseverance and a lot less about giving up and crying. As I crossed the waiting room floor in the direction of the check-in window, the door to the emergency room opened. Ivy walked through. My dopey sister didn't even see her because she was too busy moping.

"My sister's over there, if you're looking for her."

Millie, what is wrong?" Ivy said.

Millie's face lit up. "Ivy! I thought I'd never see you again."

"I didn't know I was so important to you already." She held out her hand, palm up. "Maybe this is what you thought you'd never see again."

Millie let out a gasp, but before she could take the key, I grabbed it. "I'll take that, since you already lost it once."

95

"Imagine my surprise when a key fell out of my mother's hand during the examination."

Talk about embarrassing. But it kept us from losing the key to the bad guys.

"Sorry," Millie said, "it's a long story."

Ivy handed me a business card. "If you two are around again, my mother would love a visit."

My sister hugged her.

"Millie, Jeremiah! Hurry, your dad is waiting." Mom was standing inside the door.

"Be right there, Mom," I said.

She turned and headed back out the door. I stuffed the key in my pocket.

It should be safe there.

CHAPTER 38

Millie

"Dad," Millie said "have you noticed that blue car back there?" He looked in the mirror.

"What about it?" He resumed watching the roadway in front.

"Earlier they were alongside us and I'm sure it was those men from the hospital."

"How did they go from being next to us to that far behind?" He looked in the mirror again.

"When we were at that last light they were one car behind in the other lane. Then they moved into our lane. I've been watching them for a while."

"That's why you had your little mirror out," Jeremiah said. "All this time I thought you were staring at yourself."

"It's just one of my detective tricks. Some dodo like you thinks I'm a vain female, when really, I'm spying on everyone behind me." She focused the mirror on Jeremiah. "Or some dodo right beside me."

"Max." Mom was looking in her side mirror. "He's right behind us now. Those other two cars turned off."

"I'm keeping an eye on them. You're right Millie, it is them."

"I wonder what they're up to," Mom said.

"Well, we're about to find out. They're flashing their lights and tailgating.

"Jeremiah!" Millie poked her brother in the arm. "Don't turn and look, they'll see you."

"Well, give me your little spy thing then, I'm the only one who can't see what's going on."

"Everyone got your seat belts on tight?" Dad said. "We might be in for a wild ride here soon."

Their mom looked over at him. "Max?"

"Just sit tight, Norah."

Millie's head bounced back as the car surged forward. She held her mirror up and saw the blue car keeping the same pace. Their headlights flashing, now the driver was waving his arm out the window.

They cruised at the faster speed for several miles. "Okay, everybody listen up," Dad said. "I'll make these guys think I'm pulling over for them, but sit tight. No talking and no turning around to look."

Dad let off the gas and Millie could hear the blinker clicking. She saw a bridge up ahead. The car slowed enough to pull over and stop just before the bridge. She was dying to look in her mirror. What if they had a gun?

The car shook every time a car whizzed by them going the full highway speed. She thought she heard car doors open behind them, but before she could be sure, Dad hit the gas and jerked the steering wheel to the right. All four tires squealed as they left the pavement and hit the dirt.

"Max! What about the fence?" Mom pointed to the fencing running along the highway.

The car bounced along the edge of the roadway and then dropped downhill. "Fence has been down for years by this bridge," he said, concentrating on losing the bad guys.

Dad stayed on the gas. Dirt was flying as he whipped the steering wheel to the left and they flew under the bridge, dodging rocks and debris from flash flood waters earlier in the year. Some places the back end slid so far to the right and then the left, Millie thought the car would spin all the way around.

"Hang on everyone." Dad worked the steering wheel like a pro racer, keeping them headed in the right direction. "We're taking the fun way back to Dry Brook. Hopefully, we've lost our tailgater."

"Wow, Dad, that was awesome!" Jeremiah said.

"Max, we haven't done that in years." Even Mom was smiling.

"What do you mean, Mom?" Millie said.

"When we were first dating, he scared me every time he took me out. Every bit of dirt or sand he saw, whether it was scattered on the asphalt or out in the desert, he was slipping and sliding the truck around. I was always hanging on for dear life."

Her voice was shaky and breaking up as she tried to talk over all the bumps and ruts they were flying over.

Millie and Jeremiah looked behind them but couldn't see through the dust the tires were kicking up. "I think you lost them, Dad!" Millie said.

He kept his foot on the gas, "I'm not counting on it, so we'll stay on it. Might be in for some rough spots ahead."

"Do you know how to find our way back going this way?"

"Do I know how to find our way back?" Dad mimicked her. "I was practically raised in this desert."

"Maybe we'll get some air." Jeremiah no sooner had the words out of his mouth than the car careened off a dirt ledge and soared through the air.

"Hold on!" Dad yelled, as they crashed to the ground.

"Great suspension, Dad!" Jeremiah shouted.

Dad kept the pedal to the floor, and they continued dodging ruts, rocks and bushes. The desert flew by them and in the distance they could see the realtor's office.

"Wow, that came up fast," Millie said.

"Nice little shortcut." Dad slowed the car way down as the parking lot came up fast. "Now that was a ride. Let's catch our breath so we can go into the office calmly as if it's just a normal day."

"Well, this seems to be our new normal, doesn't it Dad?" Millie said, and they all laughed together.

When they stepped out of the car, they saw Amos Lee standing on his porch.

"I'm glad you folks are here. I've got some news for you."

By the look on his face, it wasn't good.

CHAPTER 39

Jeremiah

Dad took two big steps and was face to face with the man. "What's the problem?"

"The seller is in ICU, we're not sure for how long. We don't even know if he'll live."

I let out a loud groan before Dad could respond.

"I knew it!" Millie said. "It was all too good to be true."

"Isn't this rather sudden? He lists the property and now he's in the hospital not expected to live."

Mr. Lee stammered and moved around from foot to foot. "Well, yes, it came on suddenly. But you know how heart problems can be."

"Is that what it is?" Dad pushed for info. "Was it a heart attack?"

Mr. Lee looked away. "Well, I can't say for sure." Then he looked back at Dad. "I'm not at liberty to give out that personal information."

Dad turned to talk with Mom. Mr. Lee interrupted them. "He didn't just suddenly list it. The seller accepted two other offers before yours."

"What? How can that be?"

"Well, the buyers backed out when they heard the talk about the property."

"What talk?" Millie asked. I wondered what took her so long to insert herself into the conversation.

"Millie." Mom gave her that look. The one that says shut up and let us handle this.

I looked to see how she would respond. She kept her mouth shut.

Dad followed up on Millie's question. "Can you explain what talk they heard?"

Mr. Lee hemmed and hawed. Then he chuckled, but it seemed forced. "It's just a rumor, but they claimed the property is haunted."

"Haunted?" Mom blurted out. She sounded more like Millie than herself.

"It's just a silly story, but word has been going around there is a skeleton roaming at night and people claim to have seen him at this property."

I did not trust this guy and as I looked over at Dad, I knew he was feeling the same way.

"What hospital is he in? I want to check on him."

"I'm sorry Mr. Anderson, that's confidential." Mr. Lee was wagging his head back and forth like a little kid denying he broke the cookie jar. "I can't give out that information."

"It's a matter of public record who the owner is. If you won't help us, we'll move forward ourselves."

He pulled his keys out, but before he turned toward the car he said, "I'm wondering if you have a signed listing agreement at all, Amos."

The realtor looked stunned and his eyes widened. He just stood on the porch with his mouth open.

I sure hoped there wasn't any law enforcement out on the road, because Dad was flying down the highway back toward the lodge. I could tell by the intense look on his face he had a dozen thoughts going through his head. Even Mom wasn't asking questions. I was shocked by my sister's silence.

I looked over at her. Her eyes were closed but her lips were moving. No sound came out. Maybe she's learning to think before she speaks.

"We'll pack up as soon as we get back to our room," Dad said. "I have a plan."

He hit the brakes hard when the driveway for the lodge came up. The tires slid as we hit the dirt road heading back into the Ridge Riders. After a few awesome slides, Dad got the Lambo straightened out and slowed down to the posted 10 mph speed limit.

We cruised into the parking lot just in time to see a tow truck backing up to Minnesota Mike's truck.

"What are they doing to his truck?" I yelled.

CHAPTER 40

Millie

Millie's silent praying got interrupted by the wild ride into the lodge parking lot and her brother's loud voice.

She opened her eyes to see a tow truck driver hooking chains up to M&M's truck.

"Dad?" Millie said, as everyone hopped out of the car.

She hurried over to Paisley, standing outside the office door. "Where are they taking Mike's truck?"

Paisley smiled. "It's okay, Millie. My dad is having it moved to the back lot, since he doesn't know when Mike will return."

Paisley motioned for her to step inside the office.

"Can you keep a secret?" Paisley whispered, when they got inside.

Millie's face lit up. "You bet I can. Oh wait, can I tell my brother?"

"Can he keep a secret?"

"Better than I can." At the doubting look on Paisley's face, Millie added, "I promise! I'll keep your secret."

"There were some men here earlier looking for Mike. My dad wants his truck hidden, so if they come back they'll think he's checked out." She looked around as she whispered.

"I know who you're talking about!"

"Shh!" Paisley hushed her.

"They were at the hospital trying to see Mike."

"You're kidding? I'll tell my dad. If that's okay with you?"

"Yes, I think there are weird things going on with them. I don't trust them."

Their conversation ended when Millie's dad stepped in the office.

"Hello, young lady."

"This is Paisley, Dad," Millie said. "She's my friend."

"Well, now, that was some fast friendship."

Both girls laughed.

"Say Millie, can you head on up to our room and pack?" He turned to Paisley, "We're checking out sooner than we thought."

"Oh that's sad," Paisley said. "I was hoping to get to know Millie better."

"We'll be back soon. Won't we, Dad?"

He smiled and looked at Paisley. "Yes, we'll be back. So let me settle up our bill." Millie waved good bye and hurried up to the room.

She couldn't believe what she heard her Dad say as the car headed west on the road home.

"We're coming back? Tomorrow?" Millie said. "Then why are we going home at all?"

"You and your dad and brother are coming back with the trailer and the bikes," Mom said. "I'm staying home to work."

She saw the look her Mom and Dad shared and knew there was more to it than that. She shivered from the memory of seeing Boyd Colston's name on her mom's laptop. Jeremiah looked at her.

"What's up with you?" he whispered.

She shook her head, giving him the message to be quiet. Then she mouthed "That guy."

"What?" he said out loud.

Oh brother, Millie thought, this guy was impossible when it came to secret communication. Her mom and dad were deep in a quiet conversation up front, so she whispered to Jeremiah.

"That guy I told you about, Boyd, who is messing up my adoption."

"No." Jeremiah shook his head. "He had something to do with this car."

Millie pondered that. "I don't know, I've been thinking and I'm not sure that's the reason."

"What kind of work do you have to do, Mom?" Millie asked. "Is this for Dad's company?"

"Not exactly, Millie," Mom said, and then Dad chimed in.

"You sure are the curious one, little missy." He smiled at her in the mirror, but Millie could tell something was wrong.

She felt it. There was a lot more to them heading home early than her parents were telling her.

And for once, she just didn't have the energy to question them.

103

CHAPTER 41

Jeremiah

I couldn't believe I slept all the way home. Considering we'd only had a few hours sleep the night before though, it was no wonder.

My sister was still asleep, slumped over with her face planted in her knees. I never understood how she could sleep like that. Even the sudden quiet when the roar of the Lambo engine shut off in the driveway didn't wake her.

"Millie." I could hear Mom whispering, as I hopped out of the car.

"Jeremiah, can you get the mail?" Dad opened the back of the car and took out two of our bags.

"Sure." Our mailbox stood in a barrel of fresh flowers at the edge of the yard. Neighbors said we had the prettiest mailbox on the street. That was all Mom's doing.

Glancing through the mail, I sauntered back up the driveway. A white envelope addressed to my sister stopped me cold. I couldn't believe it. She was right about that guy. The return address said Boyd Colston. The man she had been fretting about for two days.

Now, what to do? Give the letter right to Millie, or show it to Mom and Dad first? Why did I have to be the one to see this first? No matter what decision I made, I'd betray someone.

"What do you have there, Jeremiah?" I jumped at the sound of my mom's voice. She reached over and took the envelope from me, her eyes focusing on the return address.

"Mom." I touched her hands when she opened the edge of the envelope.

"What?" She looked up at me.

"It's addressed to Millie."

She glanced back at the envelope, then sighed and looked over at the car. Millie was standing outside the car and picked that moment to look our way.

"Jeremiah," Mom whispered. "Please keep this to yourself for right now."

I handed Mom the rest of the mail and agreed, against my will.

"Can you grab my bag too?" she said, this time in a loud voice. Oh brother, Mom, I thought, could you be any more obvious that you were trying to keep something a secret?

I avoided looking at my sister, but just as I bent down to grab my bag and Mom's, Millie was right there. I could feel her staring at me.

"What are you supposed to keep to yourself, Jeremiah?" Millie demanded. "What was in the mail?"

CHAPTER 42

Millie

Millie gave her brother about half a second to answer, then stormed into the house.

"Mom!" She rushed through the entryway and headed for her mom's office. "Mom!" She jumped when both her Mom and Dad stepped out of the dining room across the hall.

"Millie, let's go in here and talk." Dad turned. "Norah, will you pour me an iced tea and get something for Millie, too?"

"I don't want anything but answers!"

Dad put his arm around her as they entered the dining room. She saw him nod to her mom and knew that was his way of saying "get her something, anyway."

An envelope on the table caught her eye. She gasped when she saw the return address. Maybe she would get some answers.

Millie slumped into the chair and welcomed the cold root beer her Mom set on the table. Now she was afraid to hear the answers she'd been begging for.

"Millie." Mom sat down next to her. Dad sat at the end of the table in his usual chair. "Have you ever heard of someone named Boyd Colston?"

Millie cringed. She wanted to say no, but her mom most likely already knew. "Only when I saw him on the public records search on your computer." She looked right at her mom. "I'm so sorry. I know I'm not supposed to touch it, but I was desperate to find out what's going on with my adoption."

Mom reached over and put her hand on top of Millie's to calm her as she fidgeted.

"Okay, so you heard no one discussing that person being related to you?" she said.

Millie could feel her face forming into a snarl. "No way!" She gave in to her thirst and took a long drink of the root beer. "Thank you, Mom. This is scrumptious."

Mom took a deep breath. "Millie, what is happening, is that your birth mother is grasping for a way to hold on to her parental rights. Once those are terminated, we can complete the adoption."

"I thought she was in prison," Millie said.

"She is," her dad said, "but she can still communicate with the social worker. She also may use someone else to help her."

"Is that who this Boyd man is?" Millie looked from one parent to the other.

"It appears so," Mom said. "She is claiming that a man named Boyd is your real birth father. She says that the man named on the birth certificate, who had his rights terminated, is not your real father."

"This way she is hoping to hold open the case while they search for Boyd to do a DNA test and give her more time to fight for her rights to be retained," Dad said.

"Well, she sure wasn't interested in keeping her rights all those years ago when I first got taken away." Millie took a deep breath and looked at the only people who had been real parents to her. "She never came for one visit, and I can remember, I was five years old, and I can still remember. The foster home kept saying I would have a visit soon. But it never happened. Not when I was five. Not when I was six and by the time I was seven, I never even asked anymore when she was going to visit."

Millie's eyes were dry as she talked. She had long ago stopped crying about her birth mother. She just wanted that woman out of her life so she could be a part of this family permanently.

"Mom, they won't take me away, will they?" Now tears formed.

Dad took hold of her hands. "You're our daughter, Millie. We will fight this and win."

"Is that what Mom will work on while we're gone?"

"Yes. She'll continue her research on Boyd and also find out what's going on with the desert property."

As Millie sipped her drink, she could feel herself calming down. It made a big difference knowing what was going on, instead of wondering and worrying that the worst was about to happen.

Mom picked up the envelope and tapped it on the table. "He addressed the letter to you, but Dad and I prefer that you not open it. At least not now. We want to read it and I'll do more research."

Millie let out a sigh of relief. "That's fine with me. There's nothing anyone connected to my birth mom has to say I want to hear."

"Okay." Mom stood up and pushed her chair in. "Let's get some dinner. I'm sure we're all hungry."

"I'm starved! Did we even eat lunch today?" Millie said, as the doorbell echoed through the house. She headed to the kitchen for a root beer refill when she heard Jeremiah call out.

"Dad, you better come here."

CHAPTER 43

Jeremiah

Dad showed up just in time to rescue me from playing 20 questions. Although with our nosy next-door neighbor, Mrs. Potts, it was more like 200 questions.

"Hello, Irma." Dad reached out to shake her hand.

She put her hands behind her back, "Oh no, Max, I don't want to spread my germs. I'm getting over a cold."

I backed away from the door, around the corner leading to the hallway. While I didn't want to be a part of the conversation, I also didn't want to miss anything. I was curious how Dad would answer the questions I stumbled through.

"I'm sorry to hear you've been sick." I could clearly hear Dad from where I was standing. "What can I do for you?"

"Well, Max. I noticed a strange car in your driveway and dear me, but those look like bullet holes or something in the back window. Is everything okay with you and your family?"

"You're very observant, Irma. Thank you for your concern. Yes, we're all well." He was trying to dismiss her. I know that technique of his.

"But, Max, the bullet holes? The fancy car?" She wasn't easily dismissed. I almost laughed out loud, but that would have given away my hiding place.

"Your son says you've been out of town."

"Yes, we were away on a short business trip. We're getting ready to go out of town again, so I must get packing."

"But, Max? Why are there bullet holes in that car window? I'm scared I might be in danger."

"Nothing to worry about, Irma." How Dad could be so polite, I had no clue. "The car belongs to one of my client's and he didn't explain how they got there. Our company will repair the damage."

"Oh, I see," she said, in a voice that said she clearly did not see. "And what is it your company does, Max? All these years of being neighbors and I don't think I've ever asked you that."

I had to put my hand over my mouth to hold the laughter in. I couldn't imagine there wasn't a question she hadn't asked, and not just once, but a dozen times.

"We're in the automotive business, Irma. Thank you for your concern. I've got to get going. So much to do before we leave and I don't want to let the kids down."

"Oh, okay, well, I wanted to tell you about the man I saw..." her voice trailed off.

"Where did you see a man?" Dad's voice changed. I hoped Mrs. Potts didn't notice or she might get scared again.

"It was earlier today, right after the mailman came. It looked like he put something in your mailbox. Was there anything strange in your mailbox when you got home?"

Out of the corner of my eye, I could see my sister heading my way. I didn't look at her. She would know I was listening in and if I looked at her, she'd know it was something that concerned her. No way did I want to give her one more thing to worry about.

I was trying to remember, did that envelope with Millie's name have a stamp on it? What if that creepy Boyd guy had been to our house just before we got home? Now I was feeling a little like Mrs. Potts. Scared.

CHAPTER 44

Millie

"Mom, I'm so glad you're coming with us." Millie carried her bags to the trailer the next morning.

Mom was tucking her laptop away in the front cabinet. "I am too, honey! Dad and I realized that I can work while you three are out riding."

Millie heard a car pull up and voices out front. "Oh no, who is that?" she said to her Mom, who was rearranging the food in the cabinets. "I hope this won't ruin our trip."

"Don't worry about it, honey, it's one of your Dad's coworkers. Dad wants him to house sit while we're gone. He'll also take the Lamborghini back to their headquarters."

"We've never had someone house sit before." Millie stared at her mom. "What is going on?"

She noticed her mom kept busy rearranging food she had just put away. "Oh honey, please don't find something else to worry about." Mom still didn't look at her. "We didn't want to leave an expensive car here unattended, while we're gone."

Millie tapped her mom on the shoulder. When she turned around, she stared into her eyes. "Are you sure you're not hiding something else from me?"

Mom hugged her. "Millie, please. Make sure you have all your riding gear packed, you don't want to get out there without your helmet again."

Millie groaned. "Mom! That was only once." But she hurried out of the trailer to get her gear from the garage.

A few hours later Millie straddled her motorcycle, waiting for her dad and brother to finish getting ready. She couldn't believe they were already back in Dry Brook.

"Are we really staying for a whole week?" she said, loud enough for her Mom to hear her voice from under the helmet.

"We sure are!" Mom looked as happy as Millie felt.

"Thanks for that delicious lunch, Mom. I'm glad you came with us!" When she saw her Dad and brother kick over their bikes she pulled her start lever out and kicked it several times. The engine roared to life.

Mom stepped over to Dad's bike and patted him on the back. "You guys have a fun ride."

"We'll ride over to the lodge and see if there is any word on Mike." Dad yelled over the rumble of the engines.

Mom gave him two thumbs up and took a few steps backward as the three of them rode off.

Millie kept the throttle twisted hard as she tried to keep up with her Dad and Jeremiah. She could see them in the distance but kept her eyes on the ground not far in front of her. She glanced up every few minutes to see which direction they were going.

"Ya-hooo!" She screamed inside her helmet as she launched off a small ledge and slammed down in the sand wash. The suspension in her motorcycle absorbed the drop easily. She felt the back end slip a little, but stayed on the gas and the bike straightened out. She kept following the trails left by her dad and brother.

Millie loved the power that surged under her when she twisted the throttle harder. Even though she wasn't going as fast as they were, there was nothing like racing through the desert, hanging on and maneuvering through the sandy washes that twisted and turned. Just when she almost lost sight of them, she saw Jeremiah doubling back to check on her. When he saw her she gave him a quick thumbs up. He motioned that Dad was ahead waiting, then turned and sped away from her, leaving a plume of dust to follow.

She'd get lost riding in the desert by herself, but her Dad had grown up out here. He seemed to know where every trail led over the thousands of acres they had to ride on.

That reminded her. Maybe tonight around the campfire she could get him to tell her the story of the skeleton.

She shivered as she turned her head from side to side taking in the vast desert. She was sure what she had seen the other night could have been the skeleton Mike was talking about. But that was crazy. A skeleton walking around the desert? It sure looked real, though.

Maybe they would get to see it while they were camping. Her thoughts were interrupted as she rounded a bend on the trail and saw they were almost to the Ridge Riders Lodge.

There was Jeremiah, but where was Dad? She raised her hand questioningly in Jeremiah's direction. He pointed up and Millie laughed. Sure enough, there was Dad riding the ridge of the steep mud hill to the north of where Jeremiah was waiting. Dad was brave. Even Jeremiah wouldn't follow him up on the ridges.

Suddenly their Dad disappeared over the back of the steep hill and Millie's laughter died.

CHAPTER 45

Jeremiah

I laughed at the look of horror on my sister's face when Dad dropped off the back side of the mud hill.

"Oh Millie!" I took my helmet off to get some air. "You worry about everything."

"Well, what if he fell off the back side of the hill? Shouldn't we ride around and see?"

"Nah, he's fine. Dad rides those ridges all the time, he never comes down the same way he goes up." I hung my helmet on the handlebar and pulled two cold waters out of my fanny pack.

"Here have a drink." I handed a bottle to her. "You'll see. He'll show up any minute."

Millie took her helmet off and was sipping the cool water when her dad rode up and grabbed the water bottle.

"Hey, that looks good." He tipped his helmet back, pouring the water into his mouth through the helmet.

"Hey Dad, I've been thinking about the gold Minnesota Mike said was on our property," Jeremiah said after their Dad pulled his helmet off.

Dad shook his head. "Jeremiah, you can't put any stock in his rambling."

"But Dad," Millie chimed in. "Do you think gold has ever been found around here?"

"Yeah, and if it was, then why couldn't it be again?" I said.

Millie agreed. "And why couldn't we be the ones to discover it?"

"Yeah!" I loved that idea.

"Well, there was a story I remember my grandpa telling me."

"About a gold mine?"

My pushy sister interrupted again. "Just let Dad finish."

"Yes, oh impatient one." Dad smiled at her. "About a gold mine."

He took a few more swigs of the cold water. I could see the frustration building in Millie.

"It was back in the 1800s. There was a discharged soldier..."

"What's a discharged soldier?"

"Millie! Let him talk!"

"Well, I don't know what he's talking about!"

"He was a soldier in the Army, but then he got out. He went in search of a lost gold mine around here. He found some small nuggets on top of a steep hill he climbed. The legend talked about three buttes being near the missing gold mine. A butte is a steep hill that sticks straight up with a small flat area on top.

"Dad, can we skip the geography lesson and just hear about the gold?"

"Millie, don't you want to know why the soldier climbed the steep hill?" Dad said.

"No, because if he found the gold mine, then it isn't even missing anymore."

"That's just it," Dad said. "No one knows if he found it. He went to a big town to have the nuggets checked, and sure enough they were gold."

"Really?" Millie said.

"He got a group of his friends to go back with him to hunt for the mine. But no one ever heard from them again."

"And that's the end of the story? That's lame."

"No it isn't, Millie," I said. "That means the mine is still out there waiting for us to find it."

"Dad, could that mine be on our property?"

Dad laughed. "Well, Millie, my guess would be no. But, you never know."

"What do you mean, Dad?"

"Well, the legend says the gold mine could be in Dry Brook somewhere."

"I can't wait till we can explore every bit of that land," Millie said. "Maybe there's a butte thingee somewhere on the property and we'll find the gold."

Dad pulled his helmet back on. "You just never know, Millie. You just never know!"

CHAPTER 46

Millie

When they pulled up to the Ridge Riders Lodge, Minnesota Mike was sitting out front, like he had been expecting them.

"Now lookie who it is, come to welcome me home!" he shouted as the three of them dismounted and took their helmets off. Even Paisley came out of the office to greet them like they were old friends.

It will be great living down here in the desert, Millie thought. She couldn't wait. Well, if it really happens.

A loud bell rang on the outside wall. "Excuse me, I've got to get the phone." Paisley ran back inside as Dad was shaking hands with M&M.

Millie took that opportunity to whisper to her brother. "Did you bring that key with you?"

"It's back in the trailer in my bag."

"Wonder if he'll ask for it back?"

"I hope not, I want to find out what it's for," Jeremiah said.

"Maybe it unlocks the door to the skeleton's house," Millie whispered.

The two laughed out loud, causing their dad and Mike to look their direction. "Well, if it ain't my favorite two people in the world," M&M said. "You two act like you're discussing big business over there!"

"We sure are." Millie moved closer to her dad and Mike. "We're discussing where to ride when we leave here!"

"Oh," she added. "And we might have been wondering how you're doing."

"Is that so, young lady?" M&M let out a belly laugh.

"You're looking a lot better than the last time we saw you." Jeremiah sat next to him on the bench. "How are you feeling?"

"I'm back to my old self. They pumped me full of liquids all night. This morning I was good as new. The good folks here sent someone over to fetch me. I was jist sittin' here deciding where I should head to for my next adventure, when what do you suppose happened?"

"What?" Millie said at the same time as her brother.

"Well, doncha know?" He looked back and forth between them. "My next adventure up and found me!"

"Say Mike," their dad said. "If you're feeling up to it, why don't you have dinner with us at our camp?"

"Are you kidding me now?" He rubbed his belly. "That's an offer I'd take you up on even if I wasn't feeling up to it."

"That's great. We're camped over off Coyote Pack Trail. We're the only camp there, about a half mile off the highway," Dad said. "About 5:30 sound good to you?"

"Whatever time you say pardner and I'm there!"

"Finally," Millie chimed in. "I'll be able to hear first-hand right from you about the skeleton and the gold."

"Gold?" He looked puzzled. "Not sure where you got an idea like that, little missy." He glanced around as he answered.

"What do you mean you don't know where we got the gold idea? You..." Millie stopped in mid-sentence at the look on her dad's face.

He motioned for them to stand. "That's just fine, Mike. We'll finish our ride and head back and let my wife know we're having company for dinner."

Minnesota stood up with them, looking a little uneasy. "I'm going to take me a little snooze right now. Then I'll be fresh as a daisy when it comes time to meet you and your Mrs. for dinner." He motioned to Millie and Jeremiah. "And these young'uns too."

He turned and headed into the office without even saying goodbye.

"Dad," Millie whispered when M&M was out of earshot. "Why did you stop me about the gold? You told me yourself he kept talking about it over and over."

Her dad glanced around the parking lot and up into the balcony of the lodge before he answered. "It was clear he didn't want to talk about it, Millie."

"Maybe it's those two guys," Jeremiah said.

Millie shivered at the memory. Was someone watching them right now?

CHAPTER 47

Jeremiah

I poked a stick in the fire and watched the end flare up, then fizzle out when I held it in the air. My sister fiddled with the bag of marshmallows. It looked like she was trying to put about ten of them on the metal rod she held in her hand.

There was so much to talk about, but it wasn't safe with Mom and Dad in hearing range. After Minnesota Mike left, they said we could sit around the campfire awhile longer.

I was torn. I wanted to bounce a bunch of things off Millie, but I also wanted to hear what Mom and Dad were talking about. This had been a strange night.

"Don't be out too late kids," Mom said, before she clicked the door shut.

"Whew!" Millie let out a breath. "I thought they'd never go in."

"Me too. But I'd sure love to hear what they're talking about."

"Yeah, what was up with Mike tonight?" She scooted her chair closer to mine while she set her marshmallows on fire.

"I think he's scared," I said. "I'm telling you the other day when we were here, all he wanted to talk about was the skeleton sightings and some story about gold connected to our property."

"I wish I was as positive as you."

"What do you mean?"

"You're already calling it our property." She moaned. "It doesn't seem like that will ever happen. There are roadblocks and car wrecks everywhere we turn."

"As usual, you're exaggerating. There's only been one car wreck and look what came of that. We got to ride around in a Lamborghini!" My joke did nothing to cheer her up.

"It's just that it doesn't seem like the property deal will go through, and I don't know what's going on with my adoption."

She tossed her metal rod into the fire and we watched the

118

marshmallows sizzle and pop as the black goo dripped off the end. "Who knows? Even if we get the property, I might not even be part of this family by then."

"Come on, Millie." I hit her on the arm. "No way I'm lucky enough to get rid of you that easy."

Okay, that was the wrong thing to say. She put her head down and it sounded like she was crying. Oh man. I hate it when she cries. I was trying to make her laugh.

"Hey, now," I whispered, "I was just kidding, stop worrying. It doesn't help."

She sniffed and rubbed her nose on her sleeve. "Did you see that letter that came in the mail for me? I bet that's what you and Mom were talking about when we got home."

"Yeah," I admitted. "Did Mom give it to you?"

"They told me what's going on and said they'd rather open the letter themselves."

"What did you say?"

"I said fine." She looked right at me. "I don't know about you, but I don't want anything to do with the people I was born to. They couldn't bother to take care of me or try to get me back. Why do they have to ruin my life now when I finally have a good family?"

A look of anger replaced her tears.

"Yeah, that's a bad deal." I reached for another stick to poke around in the fire, "But look, Mom and Dad will handle it, so quit dwelling on your fears." I handed her the stick. "Here poke the fire. That's always fun."

It surprised me when she laughed at my lame joke. She took the stick.

"Besides we've got a mystery to solve," I reminded her. "Did you hear what Mike said about us being good people?"

"Yeah. What did he mean by that?"

"I'm not sure, but he said that the other day when he was trying to convince Dad the gold story was true."

"Did he tell you what he meant?"

"No. Dad was in a hurry to pack and kept shutting Mike down when he was talking about that stuff. Mike said, 'I know for certain the gold story is true but I can't tell you how I know because you're good people,' or something like that."

"Maybe he's been in some kind of trouble."

"That would make sense," I said. "Maybe he's been in jail and heard something about gold."

"Yeah! That would explain those creeps who knocked him out. They looked like criminals."

"You're right, Millie, and that's why he won't talk about the gold anymore. Remember what we heard those guys saying in the room yesterday?"

"Something about not trusting someone with information about the gold. I bet they were talking about Mike."

"And saying the old geezer needed to stop talking about the property."

"It's our property they're talking about." Millie finished my thought.

"Did you hear what you just said, Millie? You called it our property!"

Her eyes lit up. "You're right! See, I'm already more positive."

"Just don't you forget that five minutes from now! So what are we going to do about this mystery that keeps growing?"

Millie didn't answer. She was staring over my shoulder off in the distance.

"Jeremiah, look!"

Chapter 48

Millie

Millie couldn't take her eyes off the apparition, so she didn't know if her brother turned around to look. She held her breath as she watched a giant skeleton with a light glowing from the middle. It floated near the top of the mud hill, a little way, from the camp.

She stood up to get a better look and saw Jeremiah heading toward the skeleton.

"Jeremiah! Don't go over there."

He continued on. When she took her eyes off Jeremiah and looked back to the ghostly figure, she saw it moving farther away and fading. Then there was nothing there at all.

Jeremiah turned and looked at her. "Can you believe it was that close to us, Millie?" He headed back to the fire.

Millie looked over at the trailer. Her parents must not have seen it.

"Wow!" was all she could say.

"Was that what we think it was?" her brother said.

Millie sat down and stared at the fire. How could this be? Ghosts aren't real. Are they?

She looked at her brother, "Ghosts aren't real. Not even skeleton ghosts."

He didn't respond.

"Well, are they?" she insisted.

"Hush!" he whispered. "We don't need Mom and Dad coming out. We need to figure out what's going on."

"You didn't answer my question. Are ghosts real? You've been in this family longer than I have." Millie begged her brother for information. "I never even went to church before I moved in."

Jeremiah looked back over where they had seen the strange sight, then back to Millie.

"The answer is yes, and no," he finally said.

"Oh, you're a lot of help." She picked up the stick and poked it back into the fire.

"So was that a ghost? Should we get Mom and Dad?"

"I can't say for sure about the first question," Jeremiah said. "But the second one, definitely not. They'll think we've been paying too much attention to Mike and besides they'll make us come inside."

"Well, that's not a bad idea." Millie shivered. "I'm not sure I like a ghost lurking around. And what do you mean by that lame answer, yes and no?" She stared at him. "I need some answers."

"Well..." He was off to a slow start.

"Tell me the 'no' part first," Millie said. "And keep your eyes peeled behind me in case whatever that thing is shows up again." Her eyes were scanning the desert hills in the direction where they had spotted the strange vision.

"Well, I'm no expert," Jeremiah said. "But once at a church sleepover some kids were telling ghost stories, and the leader tried to explain it to us."

"Explain what?" Millie pushed for immediate answers.

"That's what I'm getting to," Jeremiah said. "But I gotta try to remember."

Millie sighed. "Okay, I'm waiting."

"Yeah, but not very patiently."

Their Dad cut his answer off when he opened the trailer door. "Hey kids, can you come in now? We're going for an early morning ride. You need to get to sleep."

Millie glared at her brother.

"It's not my fault."

She knew that. But she needed someone to blame for their conversation being interrupted.

"Come on, kids," Dad said.

CHAPTER 49

Jeremiah

Getting our conversation interrupted last night seemed worth it now. We rolled to a stop on top of a hill overlooking our property.

Dad wasn't kidding when he said early. We hit the trail before sunrise which kept the sun from blinding us as we rode east.

This was the perfect place to stop. We had a spectacular view of the sunrise in one direction. Turning our heads a little to the right gave us a bird's-eye view of the property.

"How many acres is it, Dad?" I said as we dismounted. Dad reached into his backpack and pulled out the breakfast burritos and drinks Mom had packed.

"This is an amazing view!" Millie's gaze roamed the vast property. "Oh, Dad, we just have to get this place!"

Dad smiled as he handed the food to us. "It's 1,023 acres, Jeremiah."

"Wow!"

After Dad offered a prayer of thanks, we sat in the dirt near our bikes and devoured the egg and cheese filled tortillas.

"I wish I could have seen inside the house when you and Mom toured it," Millie said. "Don't you, Jeremiah?"

"Who cares about the inside? It's all the land to ride on I care about. We can make our own tracks. And what about the shop building? Have you been inside there, Dad?"

Before he could answer, Millie interrupted, "What are those little buildings there? That one just looks like a bunch of cement blocks with no way to get in."

Dad nodded his head, "That's what it is, Millie."

"What's it for?" I asked.

"Well, the original owners of the property didn't understand that you can't build a well house until they drill the well. They got overanxious and built that block structure."

"What's a well house?" Millie interrupted. That girl could be exasperating.

"When you don't live in a city, you have to have your own well to get water out of the ground. The little building over there, about 100 feet from the block structure, is the well house. It protects the water tank and well pump from the weather. See the door on that one?"

We both nodded.

"That way you can get inside to check on the well and do maintenance."

"I wonder why they didn't just tear that other one down?" I asked.

"I don't know," Dad said. "That's what I would have done."

"I doubt it, Dad."

"Why did you say that?" Millie looked at me like I was rude.

"Because Dad never would have built it. He always checks things out to make sure he's doing the right thing."

"Good point," Millie said.

Dad yawned and pulled a ball cap out of his backpack, then laid down in the dirt. "I'll just take a little rest here." He covered his face with the cap.

"Look at those big metal containers near the well house," I whispered to Millie.

"Hold on just a sec." She dug around in her backpack and pulled out a pair of binoculars. "Let's inspect."

"Do you see locks on them?" I said, as she stared down there.

"Yes. And are you thinking what I'm thinking?"

"The key," I whispered. "I wonder if it's to one of those containers."

"But how could that be?" Millie said, "Why would Mike have a key to something on property he doesn't even own?"

"Beats me," I said. "But there is a lot of weird stuff going on."

"Yeah. Almost like someone - or something - is trying to keep us from getting this house and land."

"But why?"

"Maybe there is a gold mine and someone else wants it," Millie said.

"Then why didn't they just put an offer in to buy it?" I said. "It makes no sense."

"Well, I can't wait to ride our bikes on every inch of the land to find those butte thingees Dad was talking about and discover gold," Millie said.

I stood up and turned in a full circle to take in the desert land that surrounded us. Not too far away something moving caught my eye.

"By the way," Millie said, "when are you going to answer my question about ghosts being real or..."

Now it was my turn to interrupt.

"Hey, Millie," I said. "Look over there!"

CHAPTER 50

Millie

"That is weird. He's so close, and I didn't even hear his engine."

"Look he's still moving, but you can't hear anything," Jeremiah pointed.

"That's because that side-by-side has an electric motor. They're quiet."

They both jumped at the sound of Dad's voice.

"Dad!" Millie said, "You scared me! I thought you were asleep."

"No, I woke up just when the conversation was getting good." He smiled when she turned and looked at him.

Millie felt her heart beating hard. She wondered what he meant. What if he heard them talking about the key?

"What do you mean by that?" She hoped her voice sounded normal.

"Well, let's see." He sat up and put his hat on. "There was talk about gold and ghosts."

He stood up and brushed dirt off the back of his riding pants. "I almost thought Minnesota Mike had caught up with us." He looked over at them and smiled.

"Well, you have to admit, the stuff he was talking about can get your imagination going." Jeremiah piped up, which was a relief to Millie. She didn't want her dad to know about the key or the skeleton they saw last night.

It wasn't like they had done something wrong, but she knew her parents would want to know about both those facts.

"I was telling Millie a story around the campfire last night, about our youth leader talking about ghosts."

Millie would be forever indebted to her brother for digging her out of this hole. Well maybe not forever, but at least until he made her mad.

"How did that topic come up?" Dad said.

"It was at that guy's only sleepover, last summer at the church."

"Oh yeah," Dad said.

"Millie wanted to know what he told us, but I couldn't remember how he explained it."

"Yeah." Millie regained her ability to speak. "All he said when I asked if ghosts were real was yes and no. A big lot of help, huh, Dad?"

"Well, I can see why he'd say that. I might have answered the same way."

They both looked surprised at his answer.

He reached into his backpack and pulled out a water bottle. After taking a few sips, he sat back in the dirt and patted the ground next to him. "We're not in any hurry. Let's talk about your question now, Millie."

"Dad, I sure prefer the sound of an engine," Jeremiah watched the electric side-by-side drive down a hill and out of sight.

Dad laughed. "I have to agree with you there, Jeremiah, but some people love innovation."

"Okay Dad, what about ghosts?" Millie settled in next to him.

"First, Millie," Dad looked straight into her eyes, "I want you to remember, when you have questions about anything, you can come to us. It doesn't matter what it's about."

"Are you saying this, because of that man, Boyd?"

"Well, like the ghost question, that would be a yes and no answer."

"Oh, brother," Millie said laughing.

"What I meant is, you have a very inquisitive mind, and the tendency to worry. We want you to ask us questions rather than struggling."

Millie reached her arm as far as she could around her Dad's shoulders and squeezed him. "Thank you Dad."

"You're welcome." He patted her knee.

"Now what about the ghosts?" she demanded.

"Direct and to the point, here we go," Dad said. "If you're talking about a ghost that is the spirit of someone who died, the answer is no. But if you're talking about someone encountering an apparition, or maybe a voice that claims to be someone who has died, then yes."

Millie gasped. "Yes?" Her voice wobbled

"Demons can impersonate the dead, that's why someone might believe they're communicating with a family member or friend who has died."

"Demons!" Millie repeated. "You mean like from the devil? How do you know this stuff, Dad?"

"That's Bible truth, Millie," he said, "In a number of places it talks about deceitful spirits and demons."

"Are you kidding me, Dad? That stuff is in the Bible?"

"Sure it is," he said. "Ephesians, Corinthians, Revelation, Leviticus. It's throughout the Bible. We'll make a study of that together one day soon."

She stared at the ground without talking. Then she realized what that could mean.

"Wait a minute!" she said. "So that means if someone sees something that looks like a ghost, it might be a demon?"

She looked at Jeremiah. "That means..."

Jeremiah interrupted. "That means Dad answered the question way better than I did."

"Millie, you look like you've just seen a ghost." Dad laughed. "To use a corny old phrase."

Before Millie could answer, they heard the notification of Mom sending a text.

Dad jumped up to get his phone out of his backpack.

"That's weird," Millie whispered to her brother. "She said she'd only text if it was something urgent."

CHAPTER 51

Jeremiah

Back at camp, Dad dropped the ramp door and loaded the bikes in the trailer to keep them safe. Then he unhitched the truck from the trailer.

Mom offered to stay at camp, so we could ride the motorcycles over to Ridge Riders Lodge to meet Deputy Black, but Dad wanted her to be there. Millie seemed scared about seeing him again to talk about our wreck. I was glad Mom would be there to help if Millie got weird on us.

Minnesota Mike was out front on the same bench as before. He waved.

"Hey there!" I took a seat next to him.

"What brings you folks over this way?"

"Millie has to identify a photo for the deputy. They think they caught the man who wrecked our car."

"So they's meeting you here again?"

"Yeah, Dad told them it would be easier than coming to our campsite."

I watched to see what Dad, Mom and Millie were doing. They took their sweet time getting out of the truck. I needed to talk to Mike, but didn't want my parents to hear.

"Looks like that sis of yours ain't too keen on getting out." M&M stared at the truck.

"I'm glad my mom came along to talk her out of the truck when the deputy gets here."

I looked around to make sure no one was close by, then lowered my voice. "Say Mike, what am I supposed to do with that key?"

"What key you talking about?" M&M said.

"You know what key I'm talking about." I didn't have much time, so I wasn't happy about him joking around.

"No, sonny boy." He stared into my eyes. "I don't know what you're talking about."

The guy was nutty, I admit, but now he was making me mad.

"The key you gave us when we visited you at the hospital."

He kept staring at me. "I can't rightly say I remember that."

"Come on, Mike. You had it on a chain around your neck and said we needed to hang onto it."

M&M got fidgety and kept glancing over his shoulders. "I think you got me mistook for some other feller."

"Oh sure," I whispered as I saw the patrol car pull into the parking lot. "Just like I'm confused about the gold story."

My parents and Millie were out of the truck and heading toward Deputy Black.

I didn't want to miss out on what they were talking about, but to do that I'd have to quit trying to get the truth out of Mike. I decided to make one last attempt.

"Does that key unlock something on the property we're buying?"

"Sonny boy!" Mike startled me with his sternness. "You just don't seem to take a hint now, do you?"

He stood and shuffled off toward his room.

CHAPTER 52

Millie

Millie got out of the truck and headed toward the patrol car. The deputy was out of his car by the time she and her parents got there. She saw Jeremiah talking to Minnesota Mike and wished she could be over there.

"Afternoon, Millie."

He shook hands with her dad. "Thanks for coming here to meet me, Mr. Anderson."

"We're glad to. Thank you for tracking this guy down."

"We ran into a bit of luck," Deputy Black said. "We got some prints off the car and he did us a favor by getting picked up on an unrelated charge last night."

"What did he do now?" Millie said, anger replaced her fear.

"Millie!" Mom scolded. "That's not our business."

"Your mom's right," the deputy said and then grinned. "I'm not at liberty to talk about the drug deal they busted him on last night."

Millie decided this guy wasn't so scary. She could get through this. No problem.

"So, Millie." He pulled his phone from his pocket. "Let me know if any of these guys look familiar to you." He scrolled through the screen, tapped on it a couple times and showed her a photo, then scrolled to the next one.

She was disappointed and shook her head. "Sorry, but that isn't him."

"Neither of them?" the deputy said.

"Nope." The rat got away with it, she thought. They hadn't caught him.

Deputy Black scrolled again, bringing up another photo. Before he turned it all the way around to show her, she yelled, "That's him! I'd know that guy anywhere. That's him!"

Deputy Black smiled. "Bingo!"

"You're kidding? Is he the one who matches the prints?" Millie said.

"Sure is!"

"Mom! I did it."

"You sure did," Mom said, wrapping an arm around Millie's shoulders and giving her a squeeze.

"You deserve an ice cream," Dad said. "Great observation! All the rest of us missed seeing who was driving the car."

Deputy Black put his phone away and shook their hands. "I'll be in touch if we need anything else on this case. But looks like this guy won't be free any time soon. He had a couple other warrants out for him."

"Busy guy," Millie laughed. "What's his name, anyway? Al Capone?"

Deputy Black looked surprised. "Aren't you a little young to know about Capone?"

"Hey, what can I say?" Millie was still laughing. "I like old movies."

Her parents chuckled along with her until the deputy stunned them with his answer.

"No," he said. "This guy's name is Boyd Colston."

CHAPTER 53

Jeremiah

I couldn't believe what I heard when I joined my family by the patrol car. I hadn't heard everything, but I clearly heard the name of the driver who crashed into us.

Deputy Black was writing on the notepad he carried. He hadn't noticed the look on everyone's face.

"Did you say Boyd Colston?" It was hard not to notice Millie's strained voice.

The deputy looked at her. "Yes, that's his name." He looked from one to the other. "Does that name mean something to you all?"

"Boy, I'll say!" I couldn't believe I was the first to respond. That's loud mouth Millie's job.

"It's a long story," our Dad said. "But yes, this man has caused some problems for our family in recent days."

Deputy Black got his notepad back out. "Maybe you better tell me about it." He jotted on the pad while Dad talked. "Sounds like it wasn't a coincidence he was out here the same time as you folks."

Later we all sat around a picnic table outside the store eating ice cream. It was a rare moment when we were all quiet at the same time.

I knew what I was thinking. Maybe my worry-wart sister wasn't so wrong about everything that was happening. Something didn't seem right with this character following us around, then showing up at our house and leaving a letter in the mailbox.

"Mom? Did you guys ever read the letter that guy sent?"

Millie looked up from her ice cream. I'm surprised she hadn't thought to ask.

"No, Son," Dad said. "We haven't opened it yet."

"Aren't you curious to know what it says?" I prodded. "Did you bring it with you?"

"Yeah," Millie said, "maybe we need to see what it says."

"Now Millie." Mom reached across the table to touch her hand. "We agreed you'd let Dad and I handle this."

"Yeah, but that was before we found out the guy is tracking us down like a bloodhound." She spit the words out like they tasted bad.

"No kidding, even coming to our house," I joined in. At the sudden jerk of Millie's head in my direction, I realized I shouldn't have said that.

"What do you mean by that?" She stared at me, then turned to glare at my parents. She jumped up from the picnic bench, knocking her ice cream over. "You're all keeping secrets from me!"

Next thing I knew, I was chasing a crying shrieking Millie through the parking lot of the Ridge Riders Lodge. Oh brother, I thought, I hope Paisley isn't watching this. She'll think our family is nuts.

Too late.

"Millie?" I heard a girl's voice call out as Paisley stepped out of the maintenance building my sister ran by.

CHAPTER 54

Millie

Millie heard Paisley calling, but she didn't want to talk to anyone. Not even her new friend. She would have kept running, for who knows how long, if she hadn't tripped over a rock in the parking lot that sent her sprawling.

She heard her brother calling her name, but Paisley got to her first. All she could do was bury her face in her hands and cry.

"Millie." Paisley's voice was kind, as she knelt next to her and put her arm around Millie's shoulders. "What's going on?"

Millie couldn't talk for the sobbing. By now she heard Jeremiah's voice on the other side of her. She knew her parents were probably right behind him.

The news about Boyd still upset her, but the embarrassment of sitting in the middle of the parking lot crying got her moving. Millie stood up and wiped her eyes. "I'm fine!" She threw out her hands to push Paisley and Jeremiah away. "I'm fine!" she said again. "Leave me alone."

She hadn't counted on her mom being so close.

"Millie." That was her scolding voice. "They care about you. Don't shove them away."

Millie groaned. She hoped someday she would get control of her emotions. Not only was she angry and embarrassed, but now ashamed, too.

"Do you want to talk?" Paisley whispered into her ear.

Millie took a deep breath and forced a smile. "Thank you, but not yet. I'm sure I'm just overreacting, as usual."

Dad caught up to them and gave her a hug. "We'll work through this."

She opened her mouth to respond, but Dad shushed her with his index finger tapping her lips.

"Listen, how would you two like to go for a cruise around the desert with Paisley in their dune buggy?"

"Wow! Are you kidding me, Dad?" The question stunned Millie.

Jeremiah whooped with excitement.

"Max? Is that safe?" Oh no, hopefully Mom wouldn't put the brakes on.

"It will be fine, Norah. They'll have a long-range walkie talkie to reach the lodge if they have trouble. Eric says it's more reliable than a cell phone."

"Dad loves his walkie talkies," Paisley said.

Dad helped brush dirt off her pant legs and checked the palms of her hands like she was a little kid who fell on the playground. It felt good to let him take care of her. Crashing onto the asphalt wasn't high on her list of fun things to do. It was the second time in two days she'd done it.

"Paisley's dad came up with the idea," Dad said. "When he saw how upsetting this day has been for Millie, he offered."

"Awesome!" Paisley said. Millie wondered if the plan surprised even her.

"Eric said Paisley's been working hard, and he and Amelia are excited about new kids moving into the neighborhood. He wants the kids to get to know each other."

"That's hilarious!" Jeremiah said. "I never thought of 100,000 acres of off-road land as a neighborhood."

Paisley laughed too. "Well, there are a few humans living here and there. Just not 10 feet apart like you're used to in the city."

"Boy, am I looking forward to living in this neighborhood," her brother said.

If it happened, Millie thought. She didn't want to jinx the plan by acting like it was a for sure thing. She knew her parents and Jeremiah didn't believe in jinxing things, but she wasn't taking any chances.

"Come on," Paisley said. "Let's head over to the barn where Dad keeps the off-road toys. We've got helmets you can borrow."

"Let's meet back here by the store in about an hour," Dad said.

"Sure thing!" Millie ran to catch up with Paisley and Jeremiah.

As they drove off the lodge property, the silent little side-by-side they had seen early that morning drove into the parking lot.

"Hey." Jeremiah tapped her shoulder from the back seat. "There's that guy we saw this morning."

Millie turned around. Before she could respond, Paisley stopped the buggy and stared at the electric vehicle. "I've been watching that guy."

Why did she sound suspicious? Millie wondered.

Chapter 55

Jeremiah

"Why? What's up with that guy?" I tried to ask, but my words vanished in the wind as Paisley floored the buggy and tore out into the open desert.

We jostled around, as we sped along the desert sand washes. I was glad to hear Millie screaming and laughing. This was a great idea to take her mind off everything.

Landmarks were looking familiar and soon I was screaming with excitement just like my nutty sister. Paisley was taking us to the property. This would be my chance to sneak over the fence and try out those locks. Man, was I glad I tucked that key into my pocket before we left the trailer earlier.

The buggy roared up to the gated property and slid sideways to a halt. She obviously didn't believe in hitting the brakes until she got where she wanted to stop.

"That was awesome!" Millie climbed out and took her helmet off. I was right behind her doing the same thing.

"Here hold my helmet." I thrust it into her stomach without giving her a chance to answer. She shoved it back.

"Hold it yourself! I'm not your slave."

I tossed it into the back seat and checked my pocket for the key. "Be right back," I called over my shoulder as I climbed the fence and ran for the big metal containers. They were a lot harder to see from ground level than from the hilltop this morning. I figured if I kept running up the pathway, I would get to them.

"What are you doing?" The girls yelled at me. I kept going. I was on a mission and was about to get some questions answered as soon as I slipped this key into one of those locks.

"Jeremiah!" Millie called out. "Wait for us."

I thought about it, but if they wanted to see what I was doing, they could catch up with me. I wished I had brought a water bottle. Dad said this property was over a thousand acres, but the containers couldn't be that far from the entrance, could they?

"Jeremiah!" Millie's cries sounded more intense now. "Jeremiah!" she screamed out again.

Now Paisley's voice joined hers. "Jeremiah!"

Good grief, I thought. Why can't they just wait till they catch up with me, instead of announcing to the world I was here?

"Come see what we found!" Both voices together this time.

That got my attention.

CHAPTER 56

Millie

Millie and Paisley sat on the ground leaning against the container door, laughing, while they waited for Jeremiah.

They heard him breathing hard before they saw him. "I can't believe you ran right by these," Millie said when he appeared and dropped on the ground beside them.

"I feel like an idiot. What was I going to do? Run the whole thousand acres?"

He sat on the ground panting. "I didn't realize they were behind these big bushes. I never even looked over this way."

"What's this all about, anyway?" Paisley looked at Millie.

"Uh," Millie hesitated. She didn't know her well yet and wasn't sure how much she should say. Would Paisley think they were nuts for believing the skeleton and the gold story? She just realized, this was the first time she admitted to herself that she believed them. Or at least wanted them to be true.

"We saw these big storage containers from up on the hill this morning and I told my sister I wanted to see them up close." Jeremiah saved her from answering.

"So you run yourself ragged just to see what containers look like?"

"My brother's kinda nutty sometimes."

"Yeah, it helps me to get along with my sister."

Millie jumped up and dusted off the back of her pants. "We better get back out to the buggy, so we have time to cruise around before meeting Dad and Mom." Paisley got up too, but Jeremiah still leaned against the container. Millie could see him eyeing the padlock right next to his arm.

"I'll catch up with you guys." His panting seemed a little faked, but Millie knew what he was doing.

"Okay." She walked away, hoping Paisley would follow her lead. "But if you don't hurry, we might leave you."

"Come on Paisley! Race you!" Millie took off running. She was eager for Jeremiah to try those keys. He seemed to be feeling the same need to be cautious around Paisley.

Just as they hopped the fence and were getting their helmets back on, Millie saw the electric side-by-side driving on a dirt road intersecting the one they were on.

"Hey look." She nudged Paisley. "There's that little car again."

Paisley looked in the direction she pointed and frowned.

"Why does that bother you?"

"I don't know why. I've been seeing it a lot. He drives through the lodge property but never stops at the store or the cafe."

Millie watched as the silent little car drove onto a small fenced property and parked near a mesquite tree. The driver got out and disappeared out of their line of sight. "Maybe he's new in the area," Millie said. "Do you think he might own that property he's parked on?"

Paisley took a few steps away from her buggy to get a better view. "He might," she said. "My dad said there were some small parcels for sale over here near the big one your family is buying."

"You mean, the big one we hope we're buying."

Paisley looked surprised. "Why do you say that? My dad said your parents made an offer on it."

"I don't know what's going on with it. The realtor keeps changing the story about the property. Now he says the owner is in the hospital and might not even live."

"That is weird. I'm sure my dad would have heard something about that if it's true."

"You mean the realtor might be lying?"

"Well, I didn't mean that," Paisley paused. "I don't know, maybe I did mean that."

The girls were standing in the road laughing, when Millie saw Jeremiah heading their direction.

CHAPTER 57

Jeremiah

That was awesome how Millie picked up I didn't want to try the key in front of Paisley. She's nice enough, but right now it seems like we should keep it top secret.

I watched while they headed all the way back to the gate. You never know about ditzy girls. Sometimes they'll say they're doing something and then change their mind and do the opposite.

When they were out of sight, I dug around in my pocket for the key. Once I got it out, my hands were shaking so much from excitement, I dropped it in the dirt.

Two padlocks, one on each container. This key had to work in at least one. It had to. I was so excited I could hardly think. I'd been curious about the mystery brewing since the first day we met Minnesota Mike and heard his stories about the skeleton and the gold. The stories he claims now, he knows nothing about.

That is weird. Why is he doing that? Is he just a nutty old man getting old timer's disease? Or is there another reason he won't talk?

I struggled to get the key in the lock. The padlock was so low, my head was almost touching the ground trying to see where to insert the key. Finally, it slipped in.

Yes! I almost yelled out, but didn't want to alert the girls. So close I could feel it. The answer to the mystery was just on the other side of this big door. I hoped it didn't squeak when I opened it because Paisley might hear it from the road.

"Okay, here goes." I turned the key. Or at least tried to. No luck. Maybe the other way. "Rats!" I yanked the key out. Must be the other container.

The key slipped in. But that was as far as I got.

It would not turn either way. I wanted to kick the side of the container and bellow out my frustration, but I knew I better stay quiet. Especially since we shouldn't even be on this property. Who knew if anyone was nearby?

I stuffed the key in my pocket and jogged back to the road.

Millie caught my eye as I was hopping over the gate. She looked as disappointed as I felt.

She bounced back quicker than I did from the disappointment and surprised me by what she turned and said to Paisley. So much for top secret.

CHAPTER 58

Millie

"So, have you seen the skeleton people are talking about?"

Paisley laughed as she pulled on her helmet. "No, not yet. Have you?"

"As a matter of fact, we have."

Paisley pulled her helmet back off and stared bug eyed at Millie, then looked over at Jeremiah. He shrugged.

Thanks a lot, Millie thought, now she won't believe me.

"Where and when did this happen?"

"The most recent time was at our camp last night." Jeremiah answered before Millie could. She didn't mind, because now her story sounded believable.

"Did your parents see it?"

"No," Millie said, "they were in the trailer."

"Did you tell them about it?"

"No."

"Are you going to?"

Millie looked at her brother. "What do you think?"

He seemed to mull the idea over.

"We haven't had a chance to talk about it," she said when Jeremiah didn't respond.

"Yeah. Right after we saw it they called us to come in. Then, it's just been one thing after another."

"This is the first time Jeremiah and I have been alone to talk since we saw it."

"I can't believe this," Paisley said, but she didn't seem to doubt their story. "What did it look like?"

"Tall!" Millie shouted.

"Yeah," Jeremiah said, "and it was carrying a lantern."

"You think it was carrying the lantern, Jeremiah?" Millie looked at him. "I thought it was inside of him."

"Now that you mention it, I guess I didn't see him carrying it." He tilted his head and stared off in the distance like he was trying to remember what he saw. "But how could it just be inside of him?"

The girls laughed out loud. Jeremiah stared from one to the other. "What?"

"It's funny, because how could there even be a skeleton walking around?" Millie said.

"Yeah and if a skeleton can walk around, I guess he can have a lantern inside of him, if he wanted," Paisley said.

"It's all pretty ridiculous." Jeremiah agreed.

"Hey," Millie said, "we better get back. Mom and Dad said an hour, I bet it's been at least that."

They slipped their helmets on and climbed in. Before Paisley started the buggy, she looked over at Millie and then in the back at Jeremiah. "We have to get together again. I have to hear more about this."

Millie gave her a thumbs up and they sped off toward the lodge.

Chapter 59

Jeremiah

Paisley got her wish about getting together again sooner than we expected.

"Hey kids," Dad walked over to us as we were climbing out of the buggy. "Paisley's parents have invited us to dinner."

"Cool! Do we get to stay?" Millie, as usual, answered first.

This would be the perfect opportunity to talk with Paisley.

"You bet," Dad said.

"We'll run back to camp to check on everything and leave a light on in the trailer," Mom said. "Do you want to go or stay here?"

That was a no-brainer.

"We'll stay here, if that's okay with Paisley," I said. The big smile on her face confirmed what we were all thinking.

"I'll ask my Dad if it's okay to take you on a tour of the lodge grounds," Paisley said as our parents drove away.

"How much do you think we should tell her?" I whispered when Paisley disappeared into the office.

"I think it's okay to talk about seeing the skeleton."

"Yeah, but let's keep quiet about the gold and the key and Mike."

"Good idea," Millie whispered, just as Paisley ran out the door of the office. She was carrying popsicles.

"The benefits of your parents owning the store?" I tore the wrapper off the cherry-pineapple Big Stick. "These are my favorite popsicles in the world!"

Paisley laughed. "It is a benefit, but I have to keep a log so it doesn't mess up the inventory," she took a big lick from her popsicle. "Now let's get going, I want to hear about that skeleton!"

"What scares me most," Millie said as we walked, "is that maybe what we saw last night was a demon!" She shivered when she said it and I don't think it was because the popsicle was cold.

"Demon?" Paisley squealed. "How did we go from skeletons to demons? That sounds super scary."

I filled her in on what our Dad had told us about ghosts.

"So you guys both saw something?"

"Yes!" we said, at the same time.

"Did you say this wasn't the first time you had seen it?"

"Well, Millie said she saw it the night we were at the realtor's office, but I didn't."

"Yeah, and I know you saw something later when the tow truck was bringing us here, but you wouldn't admit it."

"It's true. I didn't see it as well as what we saw last night though."

"Wow, this is so strange." Paisley had finished her popsicle and was gnawing on the stick. "I thought the old guy was just nutty."

"What old guy?" I played dumb. "You mean the one who went to the hospital?" Millie looked over at me like I violated our oath not to talk about M&M.

"No, not him."

That was a relief, I didn't want to talk about Minnesota Mike and his part of this strange story.

"We had a guy stop in to buy ice a couple weeks ago. He was camping in the area, not too far from your property." She tossed her popsicle stick in a trash container we were passing. "He said he saw a 12-foot tall skeleton floating on top of a hill the night before."

"Did you ask him anything about it?" Millie said.

"No, I just thought he had been drinking and imagined it. He's the only person I'd heard mention a skeleton."

"Did you tell your dad what he said?" I felt a sliver of wood prick my tongue. I had chomped on my popsicle stick till it was splintering apart.

"No, it didn't seem important." Paisley looked over at me. "Didn't your dad wonder why you were asking about ghosts?"

Before I could answer, a loud gong echoed from back at the store area.

"Dinner time," Paisley said. "Let's go! Mom is a stickler for being on time."

Chapter 60

Millie

Even with their parents sitting around the campfire, Millie kept scanning the surroundings expecting the skeleton to show up again. She tried to do it without her parents noticing. No such luck.

"Millie, what's got you so interested over on that hillside?" her dad said.

Her mom and dad both looked over their shoulders in the direction she had been staring. Wouldn't that be something if he appeared right then?

"Nothing." She changed the subject. "Hey Mom, do you think you can track down the owner of the property now that Paisley's dad gave you his name?"

"Yeah, what was his name again?" Jeremiah said.

"George Smith," Dad said.

"Oh, that ought to be an easy one to search, huh Mom?" Millie tossed a stick into the fire.

"Sure." Mom chuckled. "Just have to narrow it down from 600,000 name matches."

"If anyone can do it, your mom can."

"With the address of the property and his name, we should know something tomorrow, after I get some time on-line."

"That's good," Jeremiah said. "I can't wait to learn the real story about that guy."

"Moving right along," Millie looked at her dad. "Can we talk about the journal your grandpa had for his boys' ranch dream?"

"That's a specific topic," Dad looked over at their mom. "Sounds like someone has been sharing private information with you." He didn't seem too pleased.

Millie held her breath. She didn't want to cause problems for her parents. But she wanted to know what happened to that journal.

"I'm sorry, Max. Millie and I got carried away talking about a newspaper clipping she found in that box, and one topic led to another."

"What newspaper clipping?"

"The one about the prospector and the skeleton."

Dad nodded his head while staring into the desert night. "I forgot that was in there."

He looked back at all of them sitting around the campfire. "That brings back memories. I was the same age as the kids, maybe younger, when my dad and grandpa sat around the campfire with me. Maybe even this very spot."

"Is that when they told you the skeleton story, Dad?"

"It sure is, Millie."

"Did you ever see the skeleton?"

"Nah, it's just a legend, Millie. The stuff of late night campfire stories."

"Well, we..." Millie started.

"We love stories like that!" Jeremiah interrupted and shot Millie a warning look.

She had been about to say they saw a skeleton, but obviously her brother didn't want her to talk about it, yet.

"What about the journal, Dad? Mom said it wasn't up to her to tell me about it."

"What journal are you talking about?" Jeremiah asked her.

Millie looked at her dad and then her mom, trying to decide if it was safe to keep going with this topic.

Her dad sighed. Jeremiah looked confused.

She was guessing her mom wished she had never told her anything. But the story was out now. At least some of it.

"It's a difficult story to tell, Jeremiah. I shouldn't have told Millie anything without okaying it with your dad."

"Go ahead and tell them, Norah." Dad stood and moved toward Mom. "It's okay." He patted her on the shoulder and headed for the trailer.

CHAPTER 61

Jeremiah

"Some things you just don't want to remember," Mom said as she watched Dad close the trailer door behind him.

"I have no clue what's going on," I said.

Millie surprised me. She looked at Mom. "You can tell him better than I can."

"The desert property dream started with your dad's grandpa. When he was 10 years old, he saw a movie called Boys Town."

"Hey," Millie interrupted. "I never heard this part."

"No, Millie, I guess I didn't get into all this."

"Let her finish," I said, when I saw Millie open her mouth to say more. It surprised me when she closed it.

"The movie was about a man who took care of orphaned boys. He started with five boys but eventually there were so many he bought a farm to have plenty of room. Later he named the farm Boys Town."

"What does that have to do with great-grandpa's dream?" Millie said.

"I'm getting to that," Mom shushed her. "That movie inspired your great-grandpa. He felt bad thinking about boys who didn't have a family like he did."

"You mean he got this idea when he was only 10 years old?" I thought that was amazing.

"That's where it started. It was all written in his journal." Mom stared off into the night sky for so long I wondered if the skeleton had shown up again. I looked over but saw nothing.

"Long story short," she continued. "He kept that dream his whole life, he made notes in his journal about ideas he had for someday when he had enough money to buy the land."

"Did you read the journal?" Millie asked her.

Mom smiled. "Yes, several times. Especially after your dad told me he wanted to do something about his grandpa's dream."

"Is the journal still around?" I was looking forward to reading it.

"No."

"And that's what I want to know," Millie said. "Who threw it in the fire?"

"Some years ago, before either of you were born, your dad and I spent time with kids who came from difficult situations."

Wow that was news to me. I always assumed Millie and I were the only kids in their lives.

"We'd take them to church, they'd hang out with your dad in the garage, learning about motorcycles. And a few of them we even took on desert trips."

"No kidding?" I couldn't help myself. I knew my parents had a life before we came along, but I didn't know there were kids involved.

"One boy in particular, Judson, was very difficult. We made the mistake of taking him on an overnight trip to the desert."

"What happened?" Millie said. "Is that when the journal got burned?"

Mom nodded her head. "Yes," she stared at the hillside so long it was as if she was replaying the scene in her head like a movie. "He disobeyed everything we said from the moment we got here. That night, after Judson drifted off to sleep, your dad sat by the fire reading his grandpa's journal."

Mom paused. Millie looked over at me and seemed to be thinking the same thing I was. Here it comes.

"The next morning when we woke up, Judson and one of the motorcycles were missing. It was a chilly morning, so while your dad was looking for him, I lit the fire. I didn't notice that your dad had left the journal in the chair where he'd been sitting.

"When they got back, Judson was angry because your dad scolded him and told him we were going home. As Dad cleaned up the campsite getting ready to load up, Judson must have spotted the journal on the chair."

"Did he know what it was?" Millie interrupted. Which was okay by me, because I wondered the same thing.

"Yes, he knew. Your dad mentioned the dream to some of the kids and they'd all say, 'when you do that we want to live with you.'"

"When we weren't looking, Judson picked up the journal and threw it in the fire. We didn't notice until he called out to Dad,

'There goes your old journal, you don't know nothin' about taking care of kids, anyway!'"

"What did Dad do?" I said, before Millie could get in a word. I couldn't believe a kid would do that. How could he treat my dad that way? Who was that kid? I wanted to beat him up.

"It took a few minutes for us to realize what he was talking about. I don't think either of us remembered the journal had been in the chair. By then it was too far gone to save."

"What happened next?" Millie's voice was softer than I'd ever heard it.

"Honestly, the rest of that day and the whole trip home is a blur."

"Oh, Mom." Millie got out of her chair and put her arms around Mom. "That's so sad." She knelt in the dirt next to Mom's chair and rested her head on Mom's shoulder.

I had no idea what to say or do.

CHAPTER 62

Millie

Paisley was outside watching for them as soon as they got to the lodge the next morning. Millie was the first one out of the truck, eager to see what was on the mind of her new friend. She hadn't known her long, but she could just tell she had something to say. And by that smile that wouldn't quit, she knew it was something good.

Paisley grabbed her by the hand and led her away. Millie turned to wave at her brother and Dad, "Be right back."

"Girl talk!" Paisley called out.

"Who needs it?" Jeremiah yelled back. "I'm going with Dad to see that old truck."

"You won't believe what happened here last night," Paisley whispered as the girls walked along. She looked around as she talked. Millie was still reeling from what they had learned last night at their camp, but that wasn't something she wanted to share.

"What? Tell me!"

They sat on a bench under a shade tree. Even though it was still early, she could tell this would be a hot day in the desert.

"You know that quiet little side-by-side we saw a couple times the other day?"

"Yeah," Millie whispered back to her, not sure why they were whispering. "Did you see it again?"

"I saw that and a lot more." Paisley squealed with excitement.

"The skeleton?"

"Yes! I was taking the trash to the dumpster. It was up there, hovering right above that hill."

"That's just how it was when we saw it at camp," Millie said. "On top of a hill."

"Were you scared when you saw it?"

"Well, not really scared," Millie said. "More startled. Then my brother ran toward it and that scared me. Then it vanished."

"I know!" Paisley said, "And you wonder if you imagined it."

"Exactly! What about you? Were you scared?"

"It seems like I should have been, especially since your dad said it could be a demon. But it happened so fast, I didn't have time to be. I was just standing there holding two big trash bags staring at the hill."

The girls laughed at the thought of what she must have looked like.

"It would seem like if it was a demon, we would feel terrified."

"Yeah, so if it wasn't a demon, what was it?" Paisley said.

"Is someone playing a trick?" Millie hadn't thought of that idea before.

"I saw the side-by-side twice last night."

"Hmm," Millie said. "Was it before or after you saw the skeleton?"

"Both!"

Millie gasped. "Are you thinking what I'm thinking?"

Before Paisley could answer they heard Jeremiah, "Hey, girls, get over here. Dad needs to tell us something."

CHAPTER 63

Jeremiah

"What were you girls talking about?" They looked like they'd just solved the crime of the century.

"Jeremiah!" Millie whispered. "We think we know the source of the skeleton."

"This I gotta hear!"

"Jeremiah, Millie," Dad stood near the office door. "Would you two be fine with staying here all day?"

Would we? It's the best thing I could imagine happening right now. This would give us the perfect opportunity to discuss the skeleton and maybe search for it.

"Sure Dad," I said. "What are you and Mom doing?"

"Your mom has a lead on where we can find George Smith. We're heading into the city to pay him a visit."

"Oh Dad, that's awesome," Millie said. "Maybe we can find out what's going on."

"That's what we're hoping. Paisley's parents said it's fine for the two of you to hang around here. They'll even feed you."

"You can't beat a deal like that!" I couldn't wait for Dad to drive away.

"So what's this all about?" I said to both girls as they led me over to the bench where they'd been sitting. It was far enough away from the hotel and campground no one would overhear.

"Paisley, tell him what you told me."

"Last night I saw the skeleton!"

"No kidding?"

"Yes, and just before I saw it and just after, what do you think I saw?"

Oh, brother! Girls! Why can't they just tell you something without the guessing games?

"I don't know. What?" I never play guessing games.

155

"That silent little side-by-side that's been driving around."

"You think that's connected to the skeleton?" I wasn't following her line of thinking. But if her thought processes worked like my sister's, that's understandable.

"I do."

"Why is that?" Millie asked.

"Because first he drove in through here just like he did the other day. He drove down this road and toward that hill over there."

We looked in the direction she was pointing, at the mid-size mud hill on the far side of the lodge property.

"I didn't think much of it, so I didn't keep my eye on him," Paisley said. "Plus I was struggling to get the bag out of this trash can here."

Now we looked at the big trash can next to the bench. We must have looked funny to anyone watching. Every time she mentioned a landmark, our heads turned in that direction.

"So I got the bag and was heading down the road to the dumpster and that's when I saw the skeleton appear on the hill."

"Were you scared?"

Millie laughed. "That's the same thing I asked her."

"No," Paisley said, "more startled, I think. And by the time I realized what I was seeing, it faded away. I stood there for a few minutes holding both my trash bags."

"Where did the other bag come from?" Millie said.

"Oh, come on, Millie!" I said, "like that matters."

Paisley chuckled. "It was the one from outside the store."

She looked right at me. "Look, girls like to get all the details."

I shook my head and waited impatiently for the important details. Forget that stuff that doesn't matter.

"After I dumped the trash and headed back to the store, I noticed that little side-by-side again and this time it was coming over that hill. He drove back through here and right by me."

"Did you get a look at the driver?" I said.

"No. He had a helmet on with a black face shield. I don't even know how he could see, since it was already dark outside."

"Does that guy live out here or is he just camping in the area?" I was thinking out loud and didn't expect them to have an answer, but they surprised me.

"We think we know," Millie said.

CHAPTER 64

Millie

"Well, now, lookie here, who I jist ran into."

Millie jumped when she heard the familiar voice. Paisley and Jeremiah looked just as startled.

Minnesota Mike was standing not two feet away from them. They had been so engrossed in the conversation, they hadn't seen him approach.

I wonder how much he heard? Millie thought. But then she realized it wouldn't matter, since he was the first one who told them about the skeleton. And the gold. Which he won't talk about now and they hadn't told Paisley about.

She would use this opportunity to get more info.

"Hey there, M&M!"

"M&M! I like that. I like that a lot." He patted Millie on the shoulder. "You're all right in my book."

That was enough small talk. "Hey, have you seen that quiet little side-by-side that's been driving around the desert?"

A flicker of recognition crossed his face before he jumped in with his cover-up story. At least that's what Millie figured it was. "No, I can't say as I have." Minnesota was stroking his beard and looking up in the sky as if he was deep in thought. "No, nothing like that has crossed my path."

Why won't he tell us anything? Millie wondered. She looked at her brother and could tell he didn't believe him either.

"So are you checking out today, sir?" Paisley filled in the awkward silence that hung between them. That silence when everyone knows what someone has said isn't true, but no one knows how to proceed.

"You know," he said, "I keep saying I'm only staying one more day, and doncha know, I'm gonna have to say that again today.

It's a right pleasant place you folks got here, and I think I'll stick around at least until tomorrow."

"Well, that's okay with us." Paisley must have been great at her job.

"I was just thinking on buying some ice cream for my good buddies here." He smiled and looked in Millie's direction. "You like ice cream, don't you?"

"Boy do I! And they have my favorite flavor here." She hopped up from the bench. "Let's go!"

Jeremiah and Paisley followed and as the group headed toward the store, Paisley veered off toward the shop. "You guys go ahead, I'm going to find my dad and ask if we can take the buggy out again."

That gleam in her eye told Millie just what she wanted to know. They would get to hunt for the skeleton man.

She gave two thumbs up to Paisley, and licked her lips at the thought of the mint chocolate chip ice cream waiting for her.

CHAPTER 65

Jeremiah

Paisley did a perfect job of getting us just close enough to where she and Millie had seen the guy pull in. Yet, not close enough that anyone would hear the buggy engine.

She pulled over near a large tree and shut off the walkie-talkie so it wouldn't make any noise and give us away. We all climbed out and stashed our helmets on the floor.

"Are you two ready?" I said. The plan was to hike around the edge of the fence line until we could find a good place to climb over or under. Luckily, this place had lots of bushes and trees, plenty of things to hide behind, in case we saw anyone.

The sand was thick from so many off-road vehicles racing along the road, so it made walking slow going. Millie charged on ahead. Paisley lagged behind.

Within minutes, Millie darted back. "Come on, you guys, I found a spot where the barbed wire is down. We can get through. It's right by a bushy tree to cover us."

We wandered around on the property heading in the direction where the girls had seen the side-by-side pull in. "Look here." I pointed to tire tracks.

"Let's follow them," Paisley said.

"Millie, you keep an eye out for people, I'll keep my eyes on the tracks and lead both of you."

After about 10 minutes of trudging through the stickers and bushes and stumbling into rodent holes, our efforts paid off.

"Look at that!" I said.

We all stared at the storage container in front of us. Tire tracks led up to it and disappeared. Someone had driven right into the container.

"There's no lock on the doors." I glanced over at the girls. "Let's open it!"

159

"Fine by me," Paisley agreed with Millie. "Be careful though, sometimes these doors are really loud when you pull them open."

"I'll go slow." I was already grabbing hold of the big handle and pulling it up, to free it from the latch.

Millie hopped from one foot to the other, "I'm so excited I can't stand it."

Paisley was right. The door was loud, but her idea to open it slowly worked great. The suspense was killing us.

"It's dark in there," Millie whispered.

Once the door was open, we waited for our eyes to adjust to the darkness. The little car was parked just inside the doors. The container extended probably 25 feet past the car. It was filled with junk that looked like it would be fun to explore.

"Jeremiah!" Millie said. "Look way back in there, what's hanging from the ceiling?"

We peered in, still without stepping inside, trying to make out what was in the rear. We all figured it out at once. "The skeleton!" we whisper-yelled.

"But how could that be?" I said. "That thing can't be what we've been seeing."

"Yeah," Millie said. "How would it just appear and then disappear?"

"But it has something to do with what we've been seeing," Paisley said. "It's too much of a coincidence."

"I'm checking it out. You girls stand guard and tell me if you see anyone coming."

Before they agreed and before Millie tried to push her way in, I scrambled around the car and stepped over tools and boxes, on my way to the back. Instead of watching where I was going I stared at the skeleton hanging from the ceiling. Big mistake. I tripped over a metal box and crashed down on the other side.

Cardboard boxes stacked on the floor toppled on me, as I went down. I could feel my shin throbbing.

As I was struggling to get unburied from the boxes, I heard the girls' frantic voices.

"Jeremiah! Someone's coming."

I could already hear a car approaching.

"Shut the door. I'll hide in here till they're gone," I called back. "Then run!"

CHAPTER 66

Millie

Millie was shaking as she and Paisley peered out from the bushy tree they were hiding in. The sharp twigs were poking into her skin and she wished she had worn long sleeves.

They could see two men staring at the dirt on the ground, in front of the container doors.

"They see our footprints," she whispered to Paisley, who was nodding.

"Maybe we should get farther away from here," Paisley said, "what if they follow our footprints and find us?"

Millie couldn't decide. She wanted to watch what they were doing, but it would be terrible to get caught. It was bad enough with Jeremiah inside the container.

"Come on," Paisley urged.

"I don't know. What if they hear the bushes rattling?"

"We're too far away for that."

"Even if we run farther, they might keep following the prints," Millie said. "I don't know what to do." She wanted to cry. That seemed to be her solution for every problem. Not that it ever solved anything. So it was out of the question now. "Okay." She finally agreed.

The girls shoved their way through to the back side of the prickly bush and crouched down as they broke free of the covering. They ran, half bent over, as fast as they could, to the place where they came through the fence.

Millie stopped to catch her breath once they were on the other side.

"Come on, Millie." Paisley grabbed her arm. "Let's get back to the buggy and we can get away."

"But what about Jeremiah?"

"Just for now. We'll be back for him."

Ten minutes later, the girls stared down from a plateau on a nearby hill. They watched the men back the side-by-side out of the container. Millie focused her gaze on the car parked to the side of the container. She gasped.

"I know that car!"

Paisley looked in Millie's direction. "How can you know a car?"

"Those are the men from the hospital. The ones who chased us on the way home."

"What?" Paisley yelled. "You never told me about any of that!"

"As soon as we get Jeremiah out of there, we need to talk."

The girls watched as one of the men slammed the container doors shut and latched them.

"He's spending a long time with that latch," Paisley said.

"I noticed that. What do you think he's doing?"

"I don't know for sure, but I have a bad feeling." Paisley looked over at her, fear in her eyes.

"Same here." Millie's eyes mirrored that fear. "I bet he's locking it."

CHAPTER 67

Jeremiah

While the girls were shutting the doors, I fumbled my way through the darkness trying to get as far away from the front as possible. I half crawled, half crouch-walked until I was at the far end, right under the dangling skeleton. My eyes had adjusted to the dark and I could see it was a big plastic skeleton. Sure enough, there was a lantern mounted inside his rib cage.

I heard muffled voices outside the container and the sound of someone lifting the latch. Kneeling down on the floor, I found a pile of rags and some dirty blankets. I crawled to the far corner and covered myself. Any other time I'd have thought that was disgusting, but right now the alternative was much worse.

"Someone's been poking around this place," a man was saying over the sound of the squeaking door banging open. "Did you see all those footprints?"

"Yeah!" The other voice sounded gruff, familiar and angry. Where had I heard that voice?

"I told you we shoulda locked it. It's a good thing they didn't get inside."

"How do you know they didn't?" Gruff Voice said.

"Well, look around here. Nothing looks different. If anyone broke in, there would be evidence."

They stopped talking, and it sounded like they were moving things around. I was just getting ready to sneak a peak, when I saw a flashlight beam glowing through the blankets. I held my breath, prayed and wondered how far away the girls were. They must have gotten away. The men didn't say anything about them.

"Okay, everything's okay," the first man said.

"The laptop's there?" Gruff Voice said.

Some words were muffled. It sounded like they were moving around while they talked, sometimes facing away from my direction. I needed to hear what these guys were saying, but did

I dare move enough to stick my ear out from under the blanket? Something was strange about a laptop being in a storage container full of junk.

"Yeah, it's all good. We need to go charge the battery on it before tonight," the first man said.

"Okay, grab it and let's get out of here. We don't have much time left before dark." That was Gruff Voice.

Then more from Gruff Voice. "You go in the car to find somewhere to charge it. I'll follow you. That will save time."

"And put that lock on this time!" One final word from Gruff Voice.

I heard the doors slam shut.

Now, how was I going to get out?

CHAPTER 68

Millie

Millie watched as both cars drove off the property and down the dirt road. "Come on Paisley. We've got to get down there and figure out what to do."

"Do you think it's safe to drive right up to the container now?"

"We might as well. They're gone and besides, if they come back, we can get away faster if the buggy is close by."

"Jeremiah might think it's them coming back," Paisley said.

"No, he'll recognize us." Millie had to yell over the sound of the buggy speeding up. They shot down off the hill and headed toward the container to rescue Jeremiah.

Minutes later Paisley shut the engine off as they coasted to a stop, hidden in some bushes behind the container.

"Jeremiah!" Millie yelled, as she hopped out. "Leave your helmet on, Paisley, in case we have to make a quick get away."

"Jeremiah!" Paisley joined in.

"I'm here." His voice sounded muffled. It was coming from the rear.

Millie moved toward him. "Jeremiah, can you hear me?"

"Yes." His voice was louder. He must have come out from whatever he was hiding under.

"It's locked, Jeremiah," Millie said. "Do you have the key with you?"

"What key?" Paisley said.

"I'll tell you later," Millie whispered to her. "Jeremiah! Did you hear me?"

"Yes. I have it, but what good does that do, if I'm in here with it? I've got to get out of here."

"Hold on," Millie said. "We'll look around to see if there are any vents you can push the key through."

"You think you have a key for this lock?" Paisley was persistent.

"I don't know. But it's worth a try." Millie circled the container.

"I found one!" she screamed out. "Jeremiah, come toward my voice. There is a vent down near the floor."

"Okay." She could hear him moving junk around.

"I'm here, I see it."

"Okay, shove the key through. I'll let you know when I see it."

Within a few seconds the girls could see the tip of a key.

"Yahoo!" Paisley screamed. "We see it!"

"You girls need to be quiet! Someone might hear you."

"Okay," Millie said, in a quieter voice. "I've got the key. Hold on while I try it."

"Oh man," Paisley said, "this has to work, this has to work, this has to work."

"Hush!" Millie said. "You're making me nervous. I'm shaking so much, I can hardly get the key in."

"Does it work?" Jeremiah's voice called from the other side of the container wall. "What's taking so long?"

"Millie's hands are shaking, she's having trouble getting it in the lock."

"Well, hurry!"

Millie's stomach flipped, when she tried turning the key. It wouldn't turn. Maybe the other way, she thought, but knew in her heart that wouldn't work either.

"Well?" Jeremiah yelled from inside.

"It doesn't work, Jeremiah."

"What do we do now?" Paisley looked over at Millie.

"Got any ideas, Jeremiah?"

"Does your dad have any bolt cutters, Paisley?"

"Yeah, but if we go back there without you, how are we going to explain that?"

"Let me think for a minute," Jeremiah said.

"We could just tell her dad the truth and ask him to help us," Millie said to her brother.

"No!" Paisley said.

"Why? Don't you think he would help?" Her answer startled Millie.

"Well sure he would help, but then he wouldn't trust us to go out in the buggy alone again. It's only been since you guys have been here, he's been letting me go."

"I've got an idea," Jeremiah said. "Millie, look around and see if you can find a bigger vent. We can kick it out, so I can crawl through."

"You take this side, Paisley, I'll check the other." Millie ran to the other side and within seconds shouted. "I found one! I found one!"

Paisley showed up at the same time Jeremiah's voice sounded close to her.

"Can you see it, Jeremiah?" Millie said.

"Hold on, I need to move a bunch of junk off the bottom shelf."

The girls could hear him shoving things and a few grunts and groans. It must have been heavy stuff.

"Okay, yeah, I see it," he said. "Stand back, I'll lay on my back and kick it."

Millie stepped back a few feet, just as the vent bulged out with Jeremiah's first kick.

"Millie, look over there!" Paisley whispered. "Someone's coming!"

CHAPTER 69

Jeremiah

I couldn't tell what was going on out there, but something didn't sound right.

"Jeremiah," Millie whispered. "Hide!"

I didn't stop to ask why, just shoved all the boxes back on the shelf and ran back to my hiding spot. Once again, I tripped and stumbled on the way.

I don't know how long I'd been in the container, but it felt like hours. Paisley's parents were sure to get suspicious, and I sure hoped Mom and Dad hadn't called to check in.

My heart beat hard as I crawled back under the smelly dirty blankets. I pulled them over my head, just in the nick of time.

The large metal doors screeched as the dry hinges rubbed against each other. I never heard the buggy start up, but since no one was yelling at them, I guessed they were safe. They must have hidden the buggy, too.

It sounded like someone was overturning boxes and kicking things around. Then Gruff Voice. "That stupid idiot! Can't believe he forgot the charger."

More sounds of things being tossed and kicked around. "Where the heck does he keep that thing?"

I held my breath as long as I could and then let it out before taking another deep one. I didn't want to take any chances. As mad as this guy sounded, this would be a super bad time to get caught.

"Finally!" Gruff Voice yelled. Then the sound of the doors slamming shut.

I waited for the girls to give me the all-clear sign. I was eager to get back to kicking the vent. We had to get back soon or we would all be in trouble. If we weren't already.

The minutes ticked by and I wondered just how far away they ran. But I wasn't about to come out of my hiding place. We'd already had two close calls.

Finally. "Jeremiah," Millie's whispered voice behind the container. "Can you hear me?"

I popped my head out from under the blankets. "Yes. Are they gone?"

"We think so, we'll go check. We've been hiding behind the container."

A couple of minutes passed when I heard the doors opening again. I yanked the blankets back over my head.

Oh man, they're back again, I mumbled to myself. I hope the girls got away.

"Jeremiah!" Millie's voice was clear. And loud. I couldn't believe it. She was inside.

"Jeremiah! Where are you?" Paisley said.

I threw off the dirty blankets. I never thought I'd be so happy to see my sister. "How did you get in?"

"That guy was in such a hurry, he left the lock open," Millie said.

I jumped over some debris and shoved my way around other stuff. "Come on, let's get out of here!"

"The buggy is around back, go get your helmet on," Millie grabbed hold of the big door. "We'll shut this and catch up with you."

"Oh man," I yelled out, as the buggy sailed down the dirt road and away from that property. "That is the most scared I've ever been in my life!"

"Us too!" Millie shouted over her shoulder.

I leaned forward so they could both hear me. "You won't believe what I learned though. It was worth getting trapped in there."

Paisley glanced back over her shoulder. "Yeah, you can say that now, when you're safe!"

CHAPTER 70

Millie

Millie wanted Paisley to pull over so they could hear what her brother had learned. But she knew they had to get back.

They'd been gone almost two hours.

Paisley's dad was waiting for them as the buggy pulled into the barn.

Have to act normal, Millie told herself, as they hopped out and pulled off their helmets.

"That was so much fun, Mr. Morgan," Millie gushed, hoping she wasn't overdoing it. "Thank you for letting Paisley take us out again."

"Yeah," Jeremiah said. "It was a blast!"

Paisley's dad smiled, then looked at his daughter. "That was a little longer than I expected. I couldn't reach you on the walkie."

"Oh Dad, I'm sorry," Paisley looked over at Millie with a sick look, then back at her dad. "I guess I forgot to turn it on."

"We got carried away, Mr. Morgan," Jeremiah said. "We stopped to do some exploring."

"Yeah," Millie said. "I love rocks, I can never get enough."

"That's fine, Millie. Did you bring some back?"

"Bring what back?" Millie saw her brother stare at her, like she was an idiot.

"Rocks." Mr. Morgan said.

"Oh, that," Millie tried to recover from the goof-up. "I had nothing to carry them in. And I didn't want them sliding around on the floor."

She wanted to change the subject. This lie was growing.

Mr. Morgan saved her by changing the topic. "Your parents called." He looked from Millie to Jeremiah. "They said they have good news. They're on their way back."

Millie hugged Paisley and then Jeremiah. "Yippee!" she shouted and danced around.

"I'm excited too!" Paisley said, "I can't wait for you guys to move here. I've had so much fun the last couple days."

"Me too," Millie said. "I feel like for the first time in my life, I've made a real friend."

Paisley gave her double thumbs up. "Hey Dad. How long till their parents get here?"

"Not more than an hour."

"Can we walk around and empty the trash cans while we're waiting?"

"Great idea, Paisley." He looked over at Millie and Jeremiah. "You two don't mind, do you?"

"We'd be glad to," Millie spoke up while Jeremiah nodded in agreement.

They weren't far from the store when Paisley whispered, "How did you like that for getting us a chance to talk?"

"That was awesome," Jeremiah said.

"Jeremiah, if you want to grab the bag from that can by our bench, Millie and I will get the one from the pool area. We'll meet you down the road near the dumpster." She turned back to look in her dad's direction. He was still there. "We'll be out of sight when we get close to the dumpster. There's another shade tree with a bench down that way."

Moments later, the girls listened as Jeremiah related what he'd heard the men talking about in the container.

"But what is it with the laptop?" Millie asked. "I don't get it."

"I do. It's obvious."

"Holograms!" Paisley squealed.

"Bingo!" Jeremiah pointed at her.

"Holograms?" Millie was still in the dark.

"That's how they make the skeleton appear."

"Did you hear them say that?" Millie was unconvinced.

"No, but why else do they keep the laptop in there, and they needed it charged before tonight."

"That silent little side-by-side is perfect for the job," Paisley snapped her fingers at the realization. "They can drive around, and no one hears them."

"Yes," Jeremiah continued. "They're out of sight, behind a hill like the one over there, where Paisley saw it."

"And then they project the image up on the hill." Paisley added.

"Really? They can do that with a laptop?"

"You bet!" Jeremiah nodded his head. "I've been reading about the apps you can download to do that."

"And that's why they had the skeleton in the container," Paisley said. "They photographed it to create the hologram."

They finally convinced her. "Wow!" She looked from Paisley to Jeremiah and back again. "Wow."

"Yeah, that's what I say too," Paisley's eyes were big.

"But, why would they do that?"

"That we still have to figure out," Jeremiah said.

"And what does all this have to do with our property?"

"Why do you think it has something to do with the property?" Paisley asked her.

"Because when Minnesota Mike gave us that key, he also said he had something he had to tell our dad before he bought the property." Jeremiah answered for her.

"Plus, Amos said two other buyers were scared away by the place being haunted," Millie told Paisley.

"You never told me the whole story about the key." Paisley stood up and grabbed her bag of trash. "Come on, we better finish up. Let's dump these. We have three more cans to get to."

"Yeah," Jeremiah said, "and I need some time to think through all this. I know, somehow, it all connects."

They were each lost in their own thoughts as they headed to the dumpster. They dropped the bags in the trash and turned around, in time to see the car heading in their direction.

CHAPTER 71

Jeremiah

"Come on, let's hide," I said as the car creeped along the dirt road. It looked like they were searching for something. Or someone.

"Follow me." Paisley took off through some trees that led to what looked like an RV park. She pointed to a tree with a ladder attached to it.

I looked up to see wooden planks hidden among the branches. She climbed up and looked down at us from the platform.

I looked at Millie. "You want to go first?"

"Sure, this looks fun!"

"Look," Paisley said once we were all up there. "We can watch the car from here and they'll never see us."

"This is awesome," I said, "a perfect spy tower."

"Yeah, I don't think that's what my dad had in mind when he built it, but I love to come here and watch people. It's good entertainment."

"Are they looking for us?" Millie said.

"I doubt it," I said, "they don't know we were the ones at the container. I bet they're looking for Minnesota Mike."

Millie turned to Paisley. "Have you seen him today? Or did he check out?"

"He was still here when we left in the buggy."

"I hope they don't find him." I said. "Is his truck still parked in the back?"

"Yes. When my dad told him where it was, he seemed happy to leave it there."

"I know something's up with him." I peered out through the tree branches to watch the car. "Those guys must be looking for him."

"And it has something to do with that key." Millie was right by my side.

"Will you guys tell me what this key business is about?"

Just as we finished filling Paisley in on the key and chase story, we heard the loud gong.

I looked at Paisley.

"Seems too early for dinner time. Maybe your parents are back."

Millie moved to the edge of the planks near the ladder.

"Wait a minute," I said. "Are we going to say anything to our parents about the skeleton discovery?"

"No!" Paisley said.

"Oh, that's right. Can't risk not getting to go out in the buggy."

"Maybe we can tell them later," Millie said.

"Let's get going." Paisley was already halfway down the ladder.

As we climbed down, I hoped like crazy we wouldn't run into the little car stalking the place.

CHAPTER 72

Millie

"Dad! Mom!" Millie ran screaming to her parents when they got back to the office.

She tried to embrace them both at once and Jeremiah joined in. "Group hug!" they heard Paisley calling out.

"What's the good news? What is it?" Millie burst out.

"Yeah," Jeremiah joined in. "We can't wait to hear."

"We sure can't!" Even Paisley was excited.

"Well." Dad smiled at Mom. "It's a long story, but it looks like we'll get the property."

"Yippee!" Millie jumped up and down, surprised to see Jeremiah doing the same.

"So you found the man?" Jeremiah said.

"We sure did," Mom said. "He's a wonderful older gentleman, who's been through some hard times."

"Tell us all about it," Millie said.

"Hey, how about letting your parents catch their breath?"

All three kids looked over, as Mr. Morgan approached. He shook hands with her parents and said, "Dinner will be ready in 30 minutes. Why don't you join us?"

"Absolutely," Dad said. "We're famished. We haven't eaten a bite since we left this morning."

"And then you can tell us all your news." Paisley said.

"Paisley." Her dad reprimanded. "That isn't our business."

"Actually," Mom said, "we'd love to share the story if you want to hear it."

"I want to hear it!" We looked over as Mrs. Morgan joined us.

"Mom! Millie's going to move out here. She's the best friend we've been praying for!"

Mrs. Morgan hugged Millie. "I believe you are."

Millie could feel little tingles up and down her neck. No one had ever called her their best friend before. She almost wanted to cry, but knew she needed to get over that crybaby stuff. She made the mistake though, of looking at her mom who was wiping tears from her own eyes. That was all it took.

Millie sniffed and wiped her nose on her sleeve.

"Oh good grief!" Jeremiah said. "What are you crying about now!"

Paisley jumped to her defense. "Those are tears of joy, at the thought of having me for a best friend!"

Millie was laughing and crying and nodding her head in agreement.

Chapter 73

Jeremiah

Mrs. Morgan was a fantastic cook, but I barely tasted the grilled chicken and mashed potatoes. All I could think about was what Mom and Dad would tell us. They were gushing about the delicious food and how kind the Morgans were for letting us stay there. I just wanted to yell out "Come on! Get to the good stuff." But I know better.

Finally.

Dad looked over at Mom. "I think it's time to share our news."

Mom looked at me and then around the table. If the way I felt was any sign, she saw a lot of eager faces staring back at her. Hungry for information.

"First, Mr. Smith is not in the hospital and never has been. He is a delightful 82-year-old man who lost his wife about a year and a half ago. They'd been married 61 years." Mom looked around the table as she spoke.

I groaned and looked at my sister. She looked as frustrated as I felt. Please no history, just tell us the good news. Are we getting the property, for sure, I wondered.

"Besides coping with the loss of his wife," Dad said. "He has dealt with the heartbreak of a wayward son for many years."

"What's wayward?" Millie interrupted. I swear, that girl knows nothing, which makes stories take a lot longer.

"He does bad things," I said, hoping to prevent one of my mom's teachable moments, where she takes forever to explain one word.

"Okay, keep going," Millie said. Good. She was learning.

"The son stole Mr. Smith's phone, so he never knew we had made an offer," Dad said.

"When we told him, he asked us to have the realtor mail him the paperwork," Mom said. "But we contacted Amos and

177

convinced him to drive into town tomorrow, and get Mr. Smith's acceptance or counter-offer, right away."

"Remember, that's where he asks for a different price than Mom and Dad offered." I directed my comment to Millie hoping to prevent a real estate lesson from Mom.

"How do you know so much?" Millie grumbled. I heard snickers around the table.

"I read. I listen. You should try it."

The snickers turned into outright laughter. Even Mom and Dad got a kick out of that.

"Do you think he will accept?" Mr. Morgan said.

"We feel good about it," Dad said. "He wanted us to stay and visit, and was curious about what we planned to do with the property."

"Mr. Smith was interested in our idea about using it to help kids from troubled backgrounds," Mom said.

"He showed us a photo of his son, when he was about 14," Dad said. "'This is the last good memory I have of my son,' he told us."

"What happened?" I asked.

"How old is his son now?"

"He's 42." Mom looked in Millie's direction.

"About the time his boy turned 15, he met up with a rough group of kids and started skipping school, stealing, drinking," Dad continued. "When he was 18, Mr. Smith made him join the military. He thought that would help straighten him out."

"He was hoping the strict discipline he'd learn would change his life." Mom added.

"But, he continued his downward spiral there. He got hooked up with other troublemakers."

I looked around the table and saw that everyone was as fascinated with the story as I was. Well, everyone but Millie.

"What does all that have to do with him selling us the property?" My sister interrupted.

"That's why he was so interested in us wanting to help kids. He said it would be the best thing to happen to that place, if it could help kids," Mom said.

"So the military didn't help?" I thought that would have made a difference.

"No. The son and his friends continued to cause trouble and were kicked out." Dad looked sad and it wasn't even his son.

"Dishonorably discharged," Mr. Morgan said.

"I've heard those words before!" My sister looked puzzled. "Where was that?"

That surprised me, because I hadn't, and she was the one who never knew anything.

"Where have you heard it?"

Dad and Mom were looking over at her, too.

"Oh, now I remember." The guilty look on her face made me think she wished she hadn't mentioned it.

CHAPTER 74

Millie

Millie felt her cheeks burning as everyone at the table stared.

"Millie?" Mom stared at her from across the table. "Is there a problem?"

"Well," she hesitated. "Just that, it was when I was doing something I shouldn't have."

"Maybe we should all leave," Mrs. Morgan suggested. "We're finished eating. The kids can help me in the kitchen."

"Thank you." Dad looked her way. "And we'll go take a walk."

Millie was relieved she wouldn't have to admit to snooping in front of so many people. She had hoped Mom would just forget about what she did, but here it was coming up again.

"Let's walk out by the hill where Paisley saw the skeleton." Jeremiah headed that way when they got outside. Millie shot him a warning glance, but it was too late.

"She saw what?" Mom asked, as we walked.

Millie looked over at her brother. She had enough on her hands with the dishonorable discharge. She would let him handle this.

"Well, it's kind of crazy, but she said she saw that skeleton people have been talking about. Last night. On that hill over there."

Mom looked at Dad. "That surprises me, she seems sensible enough. Why would she tell the kids that?"

"Maybe Paisley did see something." Her dad's response surprised her. This might make them forget about the whole discharge thingee.

Mom shook her head. "So much to digest here." Then she dashed Millie's hopes. "Let's get back to where Millie heard the dishonorable discharge phrase."

Millie stopped walking and sat down on what was becoming her favorite bench at the lodge. Her mom sat next to her.

"Remember, I told you I was reading about Boyd Colston on your computer?"

"Yes, I remember." So far so good. Mom didn't come unglued. Maybe she would get off with no punishment.

"Well, that was listed in his criminal background. It said dishonorably discharged from the United States Army. I didn't know what that meant."

Mom's mouth dropped open, and she looked at Dad. "You don't suppose they discharged him with Mr. Smith's son, do you?"

"It wouldn't surprise me," Dad said. "Didn't you say this Boyd character was in his 40's. They're about the same age. They both have ties to the area."

"Dad, why would the son steal his phone?" Jeremiah asked. Millie breathed a sigh of relief, with the focus off of her.

"The son was angry his father was selling the property. He thought he would inherit it someday. So he's been doing things to stop anyone from buying it."

"Like making a phony skeleton to scare people away?" Millie said. Jeremiah signaled with his eyes to keep her mouth shut.

"Like Amos told us the other day?" Millie added, to clue her brother in she wasn't giving anything away.

"He did say something like that." Dad looked over at her. "Do you remember that, Norah?"

"No. What did he say?"

"That two other buyers backed out, because the property was haunted," Jeremiah reminded his mom.

"It was when we saw him right after those guys chased us." Millie squealed.

"I remember now," Mom looked at Dad. "And he mentioned skeletons, didn't he? This is all so strange."

"That's also when Amos told us the owner was in ICU and may not live. I think Amos Lee is a liar. Maybe he is working with the son."

"No, Millie, I don't think so." Dad shook his head. "When I talked to him today, I asked who told him Mr. Smith was in the hospital. He confirmed it was the son."

"So, the son still does bad things, Mom?"

"Yes, Millie. He has been in and out of jail since his Army days."

"But Mom! What would Boyd Colston have to do with my adoption if he's mixed up with Mr. Smith's son?"

"That's a good question, Millie." Mom looked over at Dad and nodded.

"Millie, honey, we don't know. But we did something today that should get us some answers soon."

Millie could feel a tingling in her stomach. She didn't know whether it was fear or joy. But whatever it was, she couldn't talk. Jeremiah was probably happy about that.

"What did you guys do?" Jeremiah asked for her.

"We're having our attorney do a DNA test to compare Millie's DNA with Boyd Colston's," Mom said. "Then we'll know if he's telling the truth."

"But how did you get my DNA?"

"Well, once again, you forgot both your hairbrush and your toothbrush at home," Mom pretended to scold.

"Oops."

"We went home to find something of yours and those items were perfect. The attorney said Boyd's DNA is on file because of his felony arrests," Dad said.

Mom hugged Millie. "We'll have a definite answer in just a few days. Then we'll know how to proceed."

"We've hired the attorney to help us complete the adoption." Dad smiled at her.

Millie buried her face in her mom's shoulders and cried.

CHAPTER 75

Jeremiah

Millie and I had our eyes glued to the top of the hill near our campsite late that night.

"Do you think Mom and Dad would notice if we snuck up there?" I whispered.

My back was to the trailer, but Millie could see it by looking over my shoulder. "It looks like there is only one light on. I bet they fell asleep already."

"I'm sure they're tired after driving all day."

"What's the worst that can happen? They don't see us out here and they yell for us?"

"Yeah, but I hate to scare them." I struggled with the decision. "They might worry if they don't see us at the campfire."

Millie stood. "I'll tiptoe over and see if I can hear them talking."

At the trailer, she looked like she was trying to keep from laughing. She came back to the fire.

"They're asleep all right. I can hear Dad snoring."

"What about Mom?"

"Couldn't tell for sure. But I'll bet she is too."

I stood. "Let's crawl up, so no one can see us."

We no sooner reached the top than we could see, in the distance, the stealthy little side-by-side bouncing along the desert toward our hill.

"They know where we're camping, don't they?" Millie whispered.

I nodded and tried to flatten myself into the dirt. We had climbed the hill at the opposite end of where the skeleton appeared the last time. Hopefully, they would go to the same spot, or they'd find us for sure.

"They're driving with their lights off." Millie scooted closer to me. "Maybe they'll crash into a ditch."

"I hope not." I watched as they got closer. "I want to catch them in the act."

"You won't confront them, will you?" Millie sounded scared.

"No, I just mean I want to see how they do it. Then we can tell Mom and Dad and this way we're not getting Paisley in trouble."

"Yeah and not just Paisley," Millie cringed. "I don't think Dad would be too happy about us breaking into that container."

"Shh, they're almost here." I could feel Millie settling farther down into the dirt. We must have looked like snakes, slithering back and forth to move the dirt and get as low as we could. There was no moon out yet, so we were protected by darkness.

I bumped Millie with my elbow as the side-by-side came to a stop about ten feet from the back of the hill. Was that gruff voice or regular voice driving? He reached into the passenger seat and grabbed the laptop. Then he leaned down into the floor area and brought up another small device.

"What's that?" Millie mouthed as she looked in my direction.

"A projector," I whispered.

Within minutes an eerie green glow came out of the projector and the skeleton hovered just above the hillside about 50 feet from where we were.

Not squealing right then was the hardest thing either of us have ever done. I wished I had a video camera to record all this for solid proof, but I knew neither of us would ever forget what we were seeing.

"Jeremiah! Millie!" Mom's voice drifted in our direction. We turned to see her standing by the campfire. I looked back at the skeleton, but it had vanished and the side-by-side was heading back in the direction it came. Gruff Voice must have been scared away by Mom calling us.

"Come on, Millie!" I jumped up and she followed, as we ran down the hill to the campsite.

"Mom!" I yelled. "We're right here!"

We were both panting when we got back to the fire.

She didn't even ask where we had been. Her eyes were big as she stared at us. "You won't believe what I just saw!"

Chapter 76

Millie

"A skeleton?" Dad stared at Mom early the next morning while they ate breakfast in the trailer. "Are you sure you weren't walking in your sleep, Norah?"

"Tell him what you saw, kids!"

"She's right, Dad!" Millie verified. "She saw a skeleton. But it was a hologram."

"A hologram? That's just as unbelievable."

Millie told her dad what she and Jeremiah had seen the night before. Dad nodded his head as he listened.

"What made you two go up the hill?" Dad asked.

"Well," Millie looked over at Jeremiah to see if she should say more.

He jumped in. "We saw the skeleton the other night when we were sitting out there by ourselves."

"What?" Mom raised her voice. "And you never told us?"

"Well, it sounds unbelievable, doesn't it Mom?" Millie said.

"Besides Norah. If they had told us, would you have let them sit outside by themselves again?"

Dad was great, he remembered what it was like to be a kid.

"So after you guys fell asleep we went up there, in case it came back again." Millie looked at her brother for help with the story.

"Yeah," he agreed. "Even though we had seen something, it just didn't seem real."

"Ghostly images aren't real," Mom said.

"Actually, Norah," Dad looked over at her. "The kids and I had a good conversation recently about the fact that demons can impersonate dead people."

He looked back at the kids. "So that's why you two were discussing ghosts the other morning on the trail."

Millie and Jeremiah nodded. "And that's the thing, Dad," Millie said. "This didn't have the feeling of something demonic."

"What do you mean?" Mom interrupted.

"I don't know how to explain it, but I feel like, as Christians, we would sense an evil presence or something. It didn't feel that way at all."

Mom stepped over and hugged Millie. "You've come a long way in your faith, honey."

Millie hugged her back. She loved this family so much. She wished she could have the faith to believe she would really get to stay with them forever.

"So you two set out to solve the mystery?" Dad's voice brought her back to the present.

"I'm sure glad you didn't get into any more trouble than just climbing a dirt hill in your pursuit of truth." Mom squeezed her shoulders.

Millie's stomach did a flip flop. She was afraid to look at Jeremiah.

"I've got a great idea."

"What's that, Dad?" Millie was eager to change topics.

"Let's go for a ride this morning. We probably won't hear from Amos till this afternoon."

"Hey, Dad," Jeremiah said. "Can we ride over to the property again and look around?"

"And dream?" Millie added.

An hour later they rolled up to the gate. The roar of their motorcycles quieted as they hit the kill switches and climbed off the bikes.

They took their helmets off and watched Dad walk around staring at the ground. Millie could see him also looking past the gate, at the ground inside the property.

"What do you see, Dad?"

"Someone has been here."

"What do you mean?" Jeremiah stepped over to his side.

"Look at all the footprints," Dad pointed. "They start out here and then they must have climbed over the gate. They continue on the path as far as I can see."

Millie looked over at Jeremiah. He was looking right back at her. "We're dead!" she mouthed to him.

"Look at the tracks that pull up and stop here," he said. "Looks like a buggy parked here."

Who knew their dad was a tracker? No wonder he could find hidden vehicles in his job.

He looked at Millie, then over at Jeremiah. "What do you two know about these tracks?"

CHAPTER 77

Jeremiah

My heart sank into my stomach. I forgot about this lie. I was so busy feeling guilty for getting locked in the container; I forgot we came onto this property too. And without telling Dad.

What now? I wondered. What should we say? And how much? Dad doesn't know about the key either. Do we tell him?

I wondered what was going through Millie's mind. Probably double what I was thinking, the way her mind worked.

"Well?" Dad stared at both of them. "Your silence tells me a lot."

I looked over at Millie and then back at Dad.

I wanted to confess. Just not to everything. Not yet anyway. How much to confess, was the big question?

"Dad, we were so excited about the property," Millie saved me from deciding. "We asked Paisley to drive us over here and then before we knew it we climbed the gate and wandered around."

"You know this isn't our property yet," Dad said. "All three of you were trespassing."

"I'm sorry, Dad," I could barely look him in the eyes.

It didn't help that we were standing by a "No Trespassing" sign nailed to the fence post we had climbed over.

"Thank you for admitting it."

That really made me feel guilty. Because we only admitted to a tiny bit of what we had done. I needed to talk to Paisley about telling the truth. Even if it meant we all lost the privilege of going out in the buggy.

"Dad, can we stand on the gate so we can look over?" Millie asked. "That's not trespassing, is it?"

What a dork she could be sometimes.

Dad reached over and rubbed the top of her head which sure didn't help her helmet hair. "I guess we can, Millie. I'm excited myself. Who knows? Maybe by the end of the day the property will be ours."

From our view looking over the gate, we could see the fake well house, but not the containers that the key wouldn't open.

"Dad, what's that big building just beyond the phony well house?"

"That will be our shop," Dad put his arm around my shoulders. "I can't wait to get all my tools and equipment moved in there. We'll have more room than we know what to do with."

"No more bumping into each other and the bikes, like in our garage when we're trying to do stuff," Millie said.

"I'm looking forward to filling that shop with even more motorcycles." I loved working with my dad in the shop. And if there was anything Dad loved besides family, it was motorcycles.

"That sounds like a worthy goal," he agreed.

"Hey Dad," Millie jumped off the gate. "What's the first thing you'll do once we get the key to this place and it becomes ours?"

"I'd tear down that stupid looking phony well house, if it was me," I answered before Dad could get a word in.

"Well, you're welcome to do that."

"Can I help him, Dad? I love tearing things apart. Then I could make something with the broken concrete blocks."

"What in the world are you going to make with smashed up concrete?" Only my sister could get excited about broken cement blocks.

"I don't know, maybe a statue or something."

"How about a bird bath?" Dad suggested.

"Or how about a dry creek bed?" I surprised everyone with my landscaping knowledge.

Millie looked at me like I was crazy. "What are you talking about?"

"I saw it on a landscaping channel."

"Well, if I do, I'll call mine a dry brook bed, after our new home town, Dry Brook," Millie said. "But, the first thing I want to do, is hunt for the lost gold mine."

"The first thing, Millie?" Dad said. "That might take a while."

"Yeah, like a hundred years." What I really meant was never, but didn't want to upset her.

"You wanted to search for it, too."

"But not first thing, there's too much other stuff to do."

"Dad, can't I spend at least the first day searching, then move on to other stuff?"

"Tell you what. You two need to be together for either of those ideas. We'll toss a coin and see which comes first, scouting for gold or demolition work."

"I better win. Hunting for the goldmine is a lost cause. It's just an old legend, Millie."

"Didn't you read what it said in the History of Dry Brook, that Amos gave us?"

Before I could answer, the muffled ringtone for Mom sounded from Dad's backpack.

We jumped off the gate and I hurried to unzip his pack and get the phone out for him.

"Hey, Norah?"

There was a long silence. Then, "We'll be right there."

"What's up, Dad?" I looked in Millie's direction. This didn't sound good.

He was already putting his helmet on. We did the same.

"I'm not sure."

"Well, is it good news or bad news?" Millie asked.

"It doesn't sound good. Amos said Mr. Smith didn't accept our offer."

Chapter 78

Millie

Millie and Jeremiah waited on the porch step while their parents met Mr. Lee.

"What do you think will happen?" Millie turned to her brother.

Jeremiah hung his head, staring at the gravel strewn asphalt between his boots. He looked up and shook his head. "I don't know. This has been the most messed up land deal I've ever heard of."

Millie chuckled.

"What's so funny?"

"I was just wondering how many land deals you have been a part of."

Jeremiah smiled. "I guess you're right. Just this one."

Millie stood up to peek in the office window. She was dying of curiosity.

"Jeremiah! Look!"

He stood and looked in the window with her.

Their parents were hugging each other. It looked like Mom was crying. Was the news they got that bad? Millie wondered.

"The end of a dream." Jeremiah sat back down and scuffed his boots in the gravel.

Millie kept watching. "I am not giving up on Great-Grandpa's dream! He never did and neither will I!"

Then laughter came from inside the office. The door opened and their dad called out.

"Jeremiah! Millie. Come hear the good news."

"Is Mr. Smith going to sell us the property?" Millie stepped into the office first.

"No." Mom looked over at Dad. "He's not selling us the property." They had the biggest, silliest grins. But why?

Millie didn't see anything funny and she could tell by the look on Jeremiah's face, he didn't either.

Dad reached out and hugged them both. "Mr. Smith is giving us the property!"

Millie wasn't sure she heard right, but Mom continued the story. "He believes in Great-Grandpa's dream so much, that he wanted to help. So he's giving us the land."

Dad held up a set of keys. "It's ours! Right now!"

"Right now?" Millie looked at both of them and then at Mr. Lee. "Just like that? Don't you even have to sign something?"

"The detective's mind at work," Mom said to Dad.

"Sure, there is still paperwork to do. Mr. Smith is having his attorney draw up the papers. We'll meet at his office in a couple of weeks." Dad said.

"He told Mr. Lee to give us the keys today," Mom pointed at the keys in Dad's hand.

Amos stood behind his desk with a smile that matched Mom and Dad's. Maybe he wasn't such a bad guy after all. But Millie had to know one thing before she would believe it.

"Who did you talk to on the phone the night we got hit?"

"Millie!" Mom scolded. "That's not your place to ask."

"It's okay, Mrs. Anderson," Amos Lee said. "I knew your daughter seemed suspicious of me that night and I couldn't figure out why."

He looked over at Millie. "But now I understand, knowing what we do about Mr. Smith's son."

"What do you mean?" Millie asked.

"That's who called," Mr. Lee said. "Mr. Smith's son had been communicating with me regarding the sale. He called to see if you put in an offer and wanted to know if you had left yet."

"So it was Mr. Smith's son who told that guy to wreck our car," Jeremiah said. "They were already trying to scare us away."

Millie no sooner got one question answered than another one popped up in its place. But she didn't want to discuss this one in front of Amos.

"You know folks," Mr. Lee said, "Mr. Smith was not only generous to your family, but he still paid us the full commission on the property, since we lost the sale, due to his giving it to you."

"He's a very special man, indeed," Dad said. "We can never repay him."

"I have an idea how you could try," Mr. Lee said. "Mr. Smith told me today how much he misses the desert. I think he would love to come for a visit. And not just to see the desert, but to see your family settling in and enjoying the gift."

"We'll do just that," Mom shook hands with Amos. "Thank you for the idea."

Millie was growing fond of this man. She was sorry she had mistrusted him.

But she had to know how the man claiming to be her father was also involved with the desert property. What was in that letter?

CHAPTER 79

Jeremiah

"Paisley!" I yelled as soon as we got out of the truck in front of the lodge.

She looked startled to see us and came right over to where Millie and I were standing.

Her parents came out to greet ours. We pulled Paisley aside while all the parents were talking.

"We've got to tell our parents about breaking into the container," Millie blurted, before I could get the words out.

Paisley nodded her head.

"Really?" I didn't expect that response. "You're okay with that?"

"I've been feeling so guilty. My dad complimented me last night on being trustworthy with the family buggy. I felt so guilty."

Millie and I groaned. "Almost the same thing here," I said, "but wait till you hear…"

"Hey kids," Mom motioned to us to join them. "Let's head on in, they have dinner on the table waiting."

After Mr. Morgan prayed, he looked right at Mom and Dad. "Do you have news for us?"

"Boy, do we!" Millie didn't even wait for our parents to respond.

"Well, let's hear it!" Paisley poured gravy on her potatoes and passed the dish to Millie.

"Where do we start?" Mom's smile was the biggest I'd ever seen.

"How about start with the house news?" Mr. Morgan suggested. "Did you get the house?"

"Boy did we ever!" Mom said.

"I'm guessing you got a good price, then?"

Dad looked over at Mom, "You tell them."

"The seller, Mr. Smith, refused our offer," she started.

Mr. and Mrs. Morgan gasped.

"The reason he refused, is because he's not selling the property to us. He is giving it to us!"

"Amazing news, simply amazing!" Mr. Morgan stood and came around the table, patting dad on the back, then shaking his hand.

"And thank you for coming right over to share it with us," Mrs. Morgan hugged Mom. "We feel honored and can't wait to have you as neighbors."

"There's more," I said as Mr. and Mrs. Morgan returned to their seats. All eyes were on me, including Millie's and Paisley's. I'm sure they were content to let me be the one to tell.

"There sure is." Mom caught me off guard when she interrupted. "I saw the skeleton last night, and the kids saw how it was made."

I looked over at Paisley and took a deep breath. "It's now or never."

"What's that you said, Son?" Dad cut his ham into bite-size pieces while he talked.

"Last night was not when we discovered the skeleton was a hologram."

"How can that be?" Mom put her fork down and stared at me.

"I can answer that question." All of our parents looked surprised as they turned in Paisley's direction.

"Paisley? How do you know about the hologram?" Mr. Morgan stared at his daughter.

I was so glad to get that confession behind us. The girls and I headed off to what had become our bench. We were quiet as we walked.

I stood and stared at the hill where Paisley had seen the skeleton. "I sure am glad we got that out in the open." Millie breathed a sigh of relief.

"What do you think they will do?" Paisley looked back and forth between the two of us.

Our parents were still sitting around the dinner table. They said they needed to discuss what the consequences would be. But I thought they secretly looked proud of how we handled the situation.

"We probably won't be going out in the buggy for a long time."

I looked over at Paisley. "Well, we won't have time for a while, anyway. We're going home in the morning to unload the bikes and load up furniture."

"That's so awesome you're moving in right away. I can't wait."

"I can't either," Millie looked over at her. "You're the first real friend I've ever had."

Paisley leaned over and hugged Millie. And once again my dopey sister was getting ready to cry.

"Come on! We're starting a new adventure in our lives and all you can do is cry."

"Who's crying about a new adventure?" The deep voice surprised us.

We looked up to see Minnesota Mike heading our way.

"What's this I hear about a new adventure?"

"It's us!" Millie jumped up and hugged the old guy. That surprised me. But he was growing on us.

"What adventure might that be?"

"We're moving to the desert," I told him. "We got the property."

"You don't say?" M&M looked pretty happy to hear the news. "So you folks didn't let that skeleton scare you away?"

"Ha!" Millie said. "You mean the hologram!"

Minnesota let out a chuckle. "So you figgered it out, did ya?"

"Wait a minute." This guy had me so confused. "What do you mean we figured it out? You knew all along, didn't you?"

He looked around before he answered. "Well, I jist didn't figger there could be a real live skeleton walking around. 'Specially since skeletons is dead, doncha know." He threw his head back and laughed.

Millie and Paisley enjoyed the joke, but I was too busy trying to figure out how to get him to talk. He knew a lot more than he was saying.

"What is it you wanted to talk to my dad about?" I probed. "You said it was mighty important the day the deputy was here."

M&M looked over his shoulder again and then up and down the road. Then up in the sky. Stalling for time, no doubt.

"Well, it ain't my place to say anything," he said. "Besides, it will all come out in due time."

CHAPTER 80

Millie

Millie watched her dad swing the sledgehammer and hit the top of the cinderblock wall. Thankfully, whoever built this thing never went up higher than about six feet. Dad stood on a stepladder to tackle the demolition.

The block crumbled under the weight of the hammer. He swung again and again until the top row of blocks fell to the ground. Some fell on the outside and others landed on the inside.

"Dad, take a break and have some water." Millie held out a cold bottle of water when he stopped swinging and wiped the sweat off his face with his bandana.

He stepped down from the ladder and removed his safety goggles.

"Hey Dad," Jeremiah called from the other side of the fake well house. "Look at these blocks over here."

Millie stepped around to see what he was talking about.

"What is it?" She saw nothing different. The wall on the other side looked the same to her.

"I see what you mean." Dad ran his hands along the wall. "These blocks look newer than the other three walls."

"Look at the cement between the blocks," Jeremiah pointed. "It's a different shade of gray than on the other walls."

They heard a motorcycle approaching as they were studying the blocks and turned to see who was coming.

The white beard flowing out from the helmet gave it away. Soon, Minnesota Mike was pulling up next to them.

"Well, now, you don't let no moss grow under yer feet, doncha know!" M&M pulled off his helmet and hung it on the handlebars.

Dad stepped over to shake his hand. Millie reached into the ice chest and pulled out a cold water bottle for him.

"Boy you read my mind there, little missy." Mike took a long drink.

He circled the concrete structure and saw the broken bricks. "So you're taking this useless thing down, are ya'?"

"Well, for some reason the kids thought this looked like a fun project. I'm just helping them get started," Dad said.

"Yeah, but he made us work like dogs for three days first. Moving furniture and making about a million trips back and forth to the city," Jeremiah said.

"And we're only tearing it down today because I lost the stupid coin toss!"

M&M looked over at Millie. "What stupid coin toss is that, little missy?"

"I wanted to spend the day searching for the lost gold mine on our property. I read about it in the Dry Brook history. But I lost the coin toss."

"A lost gold mine," M&M looked intrigued. "Now that sounds like a worthy activity. I might want to be in on that, if you don't mind sharing some of the gold we find with an old codger like me."

"You're welcome to join them," Dad picked up the sledgehammer again. "I told them if they get this down today, they can have tomorrow to search for the gold."

"Now that's an adventure I'm looking forward to. I always suspected there was gold here!"

"That will be fun having you along on the hunt," Jeremiah crushed his water bottle and picked up his safety goggles.

"Shouldn't be a problem finishing this today." M&M chuckled as he peered over the edge of the broken blocks. "Looks like the people who built this thing made it easy for ya."

"They sure did," Dad agreed.

Millie had no clue what they were talking about.

"What'd they do? Just stack the blocks and cement them together?"

"Crazy, huh?" Dad looked over at M&M. "No rebar."

"What's rebar?" Millie asked.

"Metal rods running through the blocks," Jeremiah said.

Millie scowled. She was asking her dad. "Let me guess, you read that in a book?"

"Yeah." He grinned. "You should try it sometime."

"Hey Dad, can we knock them down ourselves now?"

"I'll do one more row, Jeremiah. Then you two can take over. Make sure you both wear your safety goggles."

"Mike, do you want to stay for lunch?" Millie noticed him heading back over to his motorcycle.

"Well, little missy, maybe I'll jist do that some other day. Right now I got me something I got to git done."

"Dad is that a concrete floor on the bottom?" Millie asked from up on the ladder as she stared down inside. "And why didn't they put a roof on this thing?"

"How is Dad supposed to know all that? He wasn't here when they built it."

"Because Dad knows everything."

Dad looked over the wall. "I'm not sure what that is. I'm guessing someone put some plywood down and then spread concrete over it. They probably didn't bother with a roof once they realized it wouldn't be needed."

"I can't wait to build my dry brook. I hope we can get this done this afternoon."

"I'm planning on knocking this wall to the ground before lunch time." Jeremiah put on his goggles and picked up the sledgehammer.

"Thanks for helping, Dad." Millie looked in his direction. "I know you can't wait to organize your shop."

"That's where I'm headed. You kids be careful. Let me know if you need me."

Millie followed her Dad to the shop. She could hear the sledgehammer crashing into the concrete blocks as she walked away. "Hey Dad, is the wheelbarrow around somewhere?"

"Sure is. Check around the back. Are you going to load up your treasures while Jeremiah knocks them down?" Dad disappeared into his shop before she answered. He was like a kid at Christmas. He loved his tools and equipment.

"Millie," Jeremiah shouted, as she was heading back. "Run back and get the pickax."

"What for?" All she wanted to do was gather up the broken blocks.

"I want to break up the floor," Jeremiah yelled.

A few minutes later she was back with the wheelbarrow and the pickax. "Who cares about the floor? Those chunks won't be big enough to use."

"Because I told Dad we'd take this down to the dirt." Jeremiah swigged a long drink of cold water.

It surprised Millie at how much progress he had made. The other three walls looked shaky with this one almost gone. They'd probably come down easy. She was glad whoever built it hadn't used those metal thingees Dad was talking about.

Millie had the wheelbarrow full, when Jeremiah started tearing into the floor.

"Dad was right," he said. "This is just a thin layer of concrete, with wood underneath."

"Hope those same people didn't build the house," Just as she spoke Millie heard the axe hit something that sounded like metal.

Jeremiah looked over at her. "Did you hear that?"

CHAPTER 81

Jeremiah

My whole body shook with the sudden stop of the axe. The first two times I swung, it dug right through the thin concrete, into the plywood and hit dirt. This time was different.

Millie appeared at my side as I dropped to my knees. "Jeremiah! What do you think it is?"

I choked way up on the axe and dug out the splintered wood and concrete to expose a large metal box. We scraped with our hands until the dirt got too hard, then used the axe to chisel dirt from around the box.

"Jeremiah! Look at that lock!"

"The key!"

"Do you still have it?" Millie's eyes were big as she stared at me.

I stood and reached into my pocket. "Are you kidding? I carry this thing everywhere."

I dropped back down on my knees and fumbled with the lock until the key slipped in easily and turned.

"Oh, Jeremiah! I'm so excited I can hardly stand it!"

She reached over and pulled off the lock. I opened the box to reveal what looked like solid gold bars. I had never seen a bar of gold, but if I had to guess, I'd say that's exactly what these were. There were numbers stamped on each one.

Millie gasped. I reached in to pick one up but it didn't budge. "Millie, these things are heavy!"

She reached in with both hands and struggled to get one out. "Feel like it weighs a hundred pounds!" Millie said.

"Twenty-five pounds. Now put it down and get your hands up!" The gruff voice came from the side us.

Millie dropped the gold bar, almost hitting my foot. We both jumped up and turned around. Neither of us had seen the little side-by-side drive onto the property.

We stared into the faces of the two men we'd been running from for days.

"You can't get away with this!" Millie yelled. I wished she would just shut her mouth as I stared down the barrel of their pistol.

"You just watch us," Gruff Voice did all the talking. "Now step aside, if you know what's good for you."

He looked over to his partner, "I told you that old coot gave the key to these brats."

Millie might have talked tough, but when I glanced over at her, I saw tears. Honestly, I felt like crying myself.

"Hold it right there!" a loud voice called from behind the men. "Put that gun down and get your hands up!"

I didn't dare take my eyes off Gruff Voice and his buddy yet. But once they put the gun on the ground, I looked beyond them.

There was Dad, approaching with a shotgun pointed right at the two men. Wow! I wanted to laugh with relief, but knew this was not the time.

Dad tossed his phone to me. "Call 9-1-1, Jeremiah!" He kept his eyes and the shotgun focused on the men.

"Jeremiah! Look!" Millie pointed down the dirt road. "They're already coming!"

Two deputy cars with lights flashing were flying up the dirt road. The white truck of Minnesota Mike followed them, bumping and bouncing along on the washboard road.

CHAPTER 82

Millie

"Dad would you have really shot those guys if they hadn't put the gun down?" Millie still sounded scared, as they gathered around the table for lunch a couple hours later.

"That sure made my day," Minnesota Mike howled. "When I pulled up there and saw you pointing that shotgun at those two fellers!" He let out one of the belly laughs he was famous for.

"Well, that would have been hard to do. The gun was empty." Dad joined in laughing. "I was getting ready to clean my shotgun, when I heard Millie shouting. I ran outside still holding it."

Millie had a million more questions but held off until Dad prayed for lunch. Minnesota Mike started gobbling down his sandwich and potato salad like he hadn't eaten in days. Millie knew she couldn't eat a bite till she got some answers.

"Where did you get that key?" she looked right at Mike. "And how did you know about them robbing that armored car and why did they bury the gold instead of spending it and why did you talk about there being gold on the property to my brother and then you stopped talking about the gold on the property and..."

"Hold it right there, little missy, now hold it one darn minute!" Minnesota Mike put his sandwich down and looked at Millie. "Can't a guy eat a decent meal, in peace, before we solve the problems of the world?"

"Not with my sister around," Jeremiah said in between bites of his sandwich.

Millie looked over at her brother. "How can you eat when there are so many unknowns?"

"Because I'm starving. Do you know how many times I swung that heavy sledgehammer. And getting a gun pointed at me took it out of me, too." He took another bite. "Besides, I have more patience than you do."

"Yes, Millie," Dad smiled at her. "Let Mike finish eating and then he can answer your questions." Dad looked over at Mike. "I don't mind saying, I'm curious about all those same things."

Millie gave in to her own hunger. She gulped her sandwich down, finishing just as Minnesota Mike pushed himself back from the table.

"Okay, listen up now, missy, because I don't want to go through this story more than once, doncha know. I'm mighty glad to be puttin' this whole sordid mess behind me. I haven't liked being involved one little bit, doncha know."

Dad and Mom were listening intently as M&M answered every question she asked, and more.

"Remember when I was tellin' you all, I had it on good authority, but I didn't want to tell you where I heard it?"

Millie breathed a sigh of relief. He really was going to tell everything.

Dad and Jeremiah nodded.

"Well, I used to drink me a bit of liquor, a little too often. There was this bar I got to hanging out in ever night, oh, about 50 miles from here.

"Well, that's where I met up with the two creeps the cops jist hauled away. And fer good, I hope.

"You know some people who are hidin' big secrets shouldn't oughta drink too much because then they start spoutin' their mouths off."

"Ohhh!" Millie interrupted. "That's how you found out!"

"Now you're catching on, little missy." M&M looked in her direction. "The one feller – what's that you called him, Jeremiah? Old gruff voice, heh-heh, that's a good one – well he's the one who took part in the hold-up four to five years ago. He was the lucky one what got away with the gold. His partner is in prison somewheres for who knows how long. These two fellers hatched up this plan way back when they was in the Army together, but they took years to get up the nerve."

"How did the gold get buried on our property?" Millie asked.

M&M laughed. "Well now missy, it warn't your property when it got buried there."

"No, but it sure is now!"

"Well, old Gruff Voice is the son of the feller who owned this place before you folks."

Dad and Mom gasped.

"He musta not known that some day his old pops would up and sell this place. When they buried the gold and added the last wall of blocks that sealed it off, he musta figured this would all be his some day.

"So's that's why he was doing all he could to scare away anyone wantin' to buy this place."

"Dad, that's why those blocks looked different on one wall." Jeremiah turned back to Mike, "How long was he going to keep the gold hidden?"

"Well, now, he had ta keep it buried until his partner got out of prison, so's they could share it."

"I didn't think criminals were that honest with each other."

"Well, now, you got a good point there, little missy." Mike looked her way again. "They ain't."

"Then why didn't the son cash it in and spend it?"

"Well, for one thing, it's got all those serial numbers on it, which is how the detectives can know where it come from. That guy jist ain't smart enough, on his own, to know how to git around that sort of thing.

"And for another, his partner in prison had another guy spying on him. If he ever did something with the gold his partner would rat him out and they'd be sharing a cell."

"Was the spy the other guy with him all the time?"

"It sure were, little missy." He held his palm up toward Millie. "But before you go firing more questions at me, the reason the spy couldn't git the gold hisself is, he didn't know where it was."

"But you did, didn't you?" Jeremiah said. "That's why you got the deputy when you saw us tearing down the concrete blocks."

"I sure did," Minnesota said. "That's one of those things that just spilled out of gruff guy's mouth when he was a'drinking."

"How did you get the key?" Millie asked.

"Well, I don't know why, but the dang fool always kept that key on a little chain clipped to his belt loop. Even boasted about it and showed me. Any smart person woulda kept the key locked away somewheres safe. One night he had so much to drink, he jist passed out there, with his head on the table. There was that key dangling down off his belt loop, jist beggin' me to take it."

He looked around at everyone at the table and smiled. "So's I took it."

"But why..." Millie started.

"Hold on there, I may be old but I knowed what you asked me earlier, jist let me finish this story.

"To tell you the truth, I wasn't so sure the story was all the way true and that's when I was talking about it myself to other people, like you folks. But the day came they busted into my room and knocked me unconscious, well then I knowed. And before they knocked me out, they let me know if I wanted to keep breathing, I better not mention another word.

"And seeing as how I enjoy breathing, and they were following me around, I made sure I never talked about it again no how, nowhere, to no one."

"Wow," Millie and Jeremiah said at the same time. Finally, Millie seemed satisfied she had heard all he knew.

"I can't believe I missed all this excitement," Mom stood and began clearing the table. "And all before lunch. What do you all have planned for this afternoon?"

CHAPTER 83

Jeremiah

I stood on the front porch looking out over our new desert property, enjoying the blue sky dotted with white puffy clouds. This was a perfect morning. A perfect life. "Thank you, God!" I shouted out to the world. Oh no, I was being as loud as my sister.

"What did you say?" I heard Millie, but I couldn't see her.

I stepped off the porch and walked toward her voice.

She was behind a big tree, about a hundred feet away, on the ground arranging her concrete chunks.

"I'm working on my dry brook." She looked up and smiled. Her face was smudged with dirt and her hair looked like she hadn't brushed it since we were tearing down the block wall yesterday. But at least she looked happy and wasn't crying.

"I thought we were going to search for the gold mine today."

She smiled. "No need. We found our gold."

"Yeah, but it's not ours to spend."

She rearranged the blocks while she talked. "I know, but that's the gold Mike was talking about all along. He didn't really believe there was a lost gold mine here. Besides, I'm too happy right now to worry about any more old legends."

"So you finally got all your answers." I plopped down on the ground next to her.

"Not all." She stopped moving chunks around and looked over at me. "Boyd."

I had forgotten about him. "It's strange, Mike never mentioned him when he was telling us everything."

"He wouldn't know anything about my adoption."

"Yeah, but even Mr. Lee said he had something to do with the property, because the crash happened after the son knew we were leaving."

"Oh, yeah, that's right," Millie moved a few more chunks around. "I don't get how he was involved in both things."

"I can tell you how." Dad's voice sounded close. We hadn't even noticed he was working on the sprinklers on the other side of the tree.

Dad sat next to us and wiped the sweat off his forehead with his sleeve. He reached over and grabbed the water bottle Millie had next to her and finished it.

"How did you find out?" Millie asked.

"Your mom got a call from the attorney this morning."

"Did he get the DNA results?" Millie interrupted.

"Didn't need to do the test," Dad said. "He went to the jail and had a talk with Boyd. He told him if he cooperated and answered all his questions, that he would represent him, at no charge, and get him a lighter sentence."

"Wow," Millie said, "what a nice guy."

"Well, let me rephrase that. At no charge to Boyd. We'll be paying for it."

"Dad!" Millie gave him a dirty, sweaty hug. "You're amazing."

"Now do you believe you can trust Mom and I to handle the hard stuff?"

I cringed. Any minute now I expected her to cry again. But she surprised me. "Yes Dad! Yes! Yes! Yes!" No tears. What a relief.

"So did he spill the beans?" I asked.

"Oh boy, did he! And there will be two people paying a heavy price for the stuff he confessed to."

"Who?" Millie asked.

"The armored car robber and your birth mom."

"How..." Millie started.

Dad laughed. "Now I know how Mike felt. Let me finish and I will answer all your questions, including what the letter said."

"You opened it?" I had almost forgotten about the letter.

"Yes, and we should have opened it a long time ago, it was good for a laugh."

"Did he say he was my dad?"

"It said, and I quote, 'I'm your real dad. Me and your mom love you. Tell those people don't buy the desert property.'"

"Are you kidding me?" Millie burst out laughing. "That's all it said."

"That's it, no 'Dear Millie' or 'Love Dad' or anything else."

"That's crazy," I said.

"Turns out that Boyd was accessing information on the dark web, posted by prisoners, looking for people on the outside to do jobs."

"Wait a minute." I was really confused. "How can a prisoner advertise online?"

"Same thing Mom asked our attorney. They have smart phones in prison."

"That's allowed?" Millie said.

"Nope but somehow they get them. That's why I said the birth mom and the robber will be in more trouble.

"It was just a coincidence that Boyd was working for both of them. The fact that the jobs involved the same people – us – made it easier for him."

"This is so unbelievable," Millie said.

"Ha! I wonder if he ever got paid?"

"And before you even ask the next question," Dad looked at Millie. "Based on this recent news, the attorney has sent a letter to the social services department demanding an immediate conclusion to your adoption. He threatened to sue them, on your behalf, for excessive delay in providing you with a permanent home, if they don't get right on it."

Millie burst into tears.

Even I felt a little teary eyed.

"Come on, Millie. That's good news, it's nothing to cry about."

She smiled over at me, tears still flowing.

"I'll tell you what you can cry about."

"What?" she mumbled.

"Mom says we've had a long enough break from school with all that's been going on. We have to get back to our schoolwork starting Monday."

"You're right," she wiped her tears and started laughing. "That is something to cry about."

CHAPTER 84

Millie

Millie stood barefoot in the kitchen, about ready to get a cold drink, when she heard a car approach. Hurrying over to the window, she saw the deputy they'd become friends with. Someone else was in the car with him.

Her dad opened the front door as she was slipping on her shoes. "Norah, Millie. Deputy Black has news for us."

When they got outside, Millie saw a little boy. He stared at the ground, kicking the dirt with the toe of his left foot. His shoelaces were raggedy and untied.

"Millie and Jeremiah, congratulations on solving the armored car theft." Deputy Black shook their hands. "There will be a formal ceremony next month at the Sheriff's office with the president of the armored car company."

"Oh, wow!" Millie looked at her brother and then back to the deputy. "Are you kidding?"

"There is also a reward."

"And this morning I thought life couldn't get any better," Jeremiah looked at Millie. "I guess we really struck gold!"

While they laughed together, Deputy Black put his arm around the boy. "Now, my second reason for dropping by. This is Caleb."

Jeremiah greeted him.

"Hey, Caleb," Millie joined in. "What's that you've got there?"

Caleb showed her a crumpled photo. It was a quad rider racing through the desert.

"Hey," Millie took the photo from him to get a better look. "Number 37. He looks fast."

Caleb smiled and pointed to the deputy.

"Is that him riding?" Millie looked over at Deputy Black.

"Uh-huh," Caleb whispered. "He's nice."

"His mom is going through a hard time," Deputy Black looked at her parents. "She'll be going away for a few months."

Millie wondered if that meant jail.

"Jeremiah," Dad held out his keys. "Why don't you take Caleb down to the shop and let him sit on your motorcycle?"

The deputy waited for them to leave. "I hate to get child protective services involved. His mom asked if I would find someone to take care of him."

"Do you have anyone in mind?" Mom asked.

"No, but I know you're praying folks, so I wanted to ask you to pray about finding a family."

"Are you a believer?" Dad asked.

"I'm trying to be, Max, but it's hard. When I see kids who've been mistreated and abused." He stared up in the sky, then looked back at Dad. "Where is God in all of this?"

Millie could hardly breathe. It was a question she had struggled with most of her life. She really needed to hear Dad's answer.

He looked in her direction. She hoped he wouldn't send her to the shop too.

"Millie, run inside and get my Bible."

When she returned, he touched her shoulder. "Stay right here."

"I don't have all the answers. But I can tell you a few things." He held his Bible out. "First, this book tells me that Jesus loves me and it is filled with promises for those of us who have given our lives to Him."

He stepped behind Millie, placing a hand on her shoulder. "The second thing I will tell you, is about this special young lady. When I think..." he paused. It sounded like he was sniffing. She heard him inhale deeply then slowly breathe out. "When I think of all that she has gone through and the evil she has seen, it breaks my heart and I wonder, just like you, where was God?"

Millie turned. "Oh, Dad! I didn't know you felt that way," she said through tears while hugging him. Then Millie stepped back and wiped her eyes, wanting to hear more. She needed an answer for the question that had haunted her.

Her dad continued. "When I was ten, my grandpa died. He had been in a coma for a few days but one afternoon, I saw tears on his cheeks. Then he mumbled something and became animated."

Dad took another deep breath. "I believe Grandpa saw the angels coming to take him to heaven. Just like the Bible promises us."

"Is that when he died?"

"Yes, Millie, and it was an amazing experience to be there."

Dad looked back at the deputy. "I don't understand why God doesn't stop the evil from hurting the children and it breaks my heart. But I will not let that evil also destroy my faith in Jesus."

"Trust in the Lord with all your heart," Millie said. "just like you taught me the Bible says."

"What did your Grandpa say there at the end?" Deputy Black asked.

"He said, 'Don't forget the dream, Max.'"

"What was he talking about?"

"I know!" Millie said. "He was talking about the dream to buy the land and take care of kids."

"That's right, Millie," Dad put his arm around her shoulders and pulled her close.

"So it was your grandpa's dream to help kids like Caleb? Do you suppose God led me here to talk to you about Caleb?"

Dad looked up in the sky and mouthed the words, "Thank you, God!"

"I bet your grandpa would be dancing up a storm if he knew about Caleb!" Millie said.

"Absolutely!" Mom agreed and looked at Deputy Black, then over at Dad.

"Let's all go tell Caleb the news."

Thank you for coming along on

Jeremiah and Millie's adventures in

The Skeleton and the Lantern

Please leave a review
on Amazon.com

MotoMysteries

Book 1 - The Skeleton and the Lantern

Book 2 - Ghost Lights of Dry Brook (Spring 2020)

Book 3 - Phantom Ship in the Desert (Fall 2020)

Visit www.sherrikukla.com regularly for updates on new books

ABOUT THE AUTHOR

Sherri Kukla and her husband Steve are the publishers of *S&S Off Road Magazine* (www.ssorm.com) and the founders and directors of Thundering Trails off road camp for kids.

Acknowledgements

I am especially grateful for those who helped bring this story to life:

Deputy Sheriff Larry Hammers for answering questions about law enforcement. Realtor John Elliott helped me to understand real estate deals. Science and math teacher David Woltz for providing logistical information.

Justinna Kukla and Jana Foley read the completed manuscript and gave valuable feedback. An extra measure of thanks to my Aunt Jana for letting me bounce hundreds of ideas off of her as the project drew to a close.

My sister, Regina Jensen, for prayer support throughout the project. My sons Byron and Charlie Kukla for discussing plot ideas with me.

My husband, Steve, for 45 awesome years of adventures to draw on for story ideas and for surprising me by reading the entire manuscript and marking it all up to make it better.

Finally all the praise to God for inspiration and creativity and for His wondrous gift of salvation and abundant life.

In Memory of Black

May 2, 2013 - March 23, 2019

K9 Partner of
San Diego County
Deputy Sheriff Larry Hammers

Made in the USA
San Bernardino,
CA